Twelve Dates
'Till Christmas

Jennifer C. Wilson

ACKNOWLEDGEMENTS

This is my first fully contemporary-set story, and I'm so grateful to my fellow Ocelots who provided feedback on the idea, completed manuscript, cover and blurb, to help me bring it to life: Vanessa Couchman; Cathie Dunn; Nancy Jardine; and Yvonne Marjot. Extra thanks to Sue Barnard, for once again waving her editorial magic wand, and to Laurence Patterson for creating a cover which I think suits the story perfectly.

CONTENTS

ABOUT THE AUTHOR

Jennifer has been stalking dead monarchs since she was a child. It started with Mary, Queen of Scots, then moved onto Richard III. At least now it results in a story!

She won North Tyneside Libraries' Story Tyne short story competition in 2014 (no dead monarchs, but still not a cheerful read), and has been filling notebooks and hard-drives ever since. Her Kindred Spirits series, following the 'lives' of some very interesting ghostly communities, is published by Darkstroke, and her historical romances by Ocelot Press.

Twelve Dates 'Till Christmas is her first contemporary romance, but most likely not her last…

You can find her online at:
Facebook:
https://www.facebook.com/jennifercwilsonwriter/
Twitter:
https://twitter.com/inkjunkie1984
Website:
https://jennifercwilsonwriter.wordpress.com/
Instagram:
https://www.instagram.com/jennifercwilsonwriter/
Amazon (UK):
https://www.amazon.co.uk/Jennifer-C-Wilson/e/B018UBP1ZO/
Amazon (US):
https://www.amazon.com/Jennifer-C-Wilson/e/B018UBP1ZO/

SATURDAY 5TH OCTOBER

Lexie

"Lex! Come on! The car's waiting outside; will you get a move on?"

With a final glance in the mirror, Lexie Carmichael rolled her eyes, grabbed her handbag, and hurried from her bedroom to the front door before Callum marched in and physically dragged her into the lift lobby. By the time she had locked up he was holding the lift doors open, clearly fighting the urge to look at his watch for the umpteenth time since they had heard the taxi outside beep its horn. It was his fault they were running late anyway; if he hadn't opened a bottle of wine as soon as he sauntered into her kitchen, she would easily have been ready just minutes after he'd arrived, and they could have waited patiently for the taxi, without any hassle at all. But no, with snacks and wine in hand, Callum had settled himself comfortably on Lexie's bed as she made the finishing touches to her hair, make-up and jewellery, both completely losing track of time as he distracted and delayed her with gossip. The boy spent so much time gossiping that he would be late for his own funeral.

Still, at least her efforts hadn't been wasted. As the taxi

pulled up outside the sweeping entrance to the St Pancras Hotel, Lexie knew that she was looking her best, and as always, Callum would be looking his handsome self on her arm. To anyone who didn't know, they looked the perfect couple, as they got out of the car and made their way through the main reception of the hotel.

Callum, acting the gentleman as always, rushed two steps ahead of her to pull open the door to the ballroom, where two of their closest friends from university were celebrating the announcement of their engagement that evening. Lexie smiled at him; this was their second party in the same room in less than a month, having celebrated Callum's thirtieth birthday there just a few weeks earlier.

"See, still quiet, we were nowhere near being late," she said, as Callum took her jacket and handed it in to the cloakroom for her.

"Ah, but it's never worth the risk," he replied, before cocking his head towards the bar. "Usual?"

Her nod was greeted by the arrival of a glass of rosé a few minutes later, as Callum found her at a table, chatting away happily to a gaggle of friends from their student days.

"And here's your worse half," said Sam, rising to clap Callum's shoulder in greeting. "Honestly, I don't know why you don't just put us all out of our misery and book your own engagement party, make the whole 'Mr and Mrs Fitzpatrick' thing official."

Lexie rolled her eyes. "Sam, that wasn't funny back then, and it isn't funny now." Twelve years, she thought; twelve years she had been sitting through these comments.

"Besides," Callum chimed in, taking the empty seat beside Lexie, "if Lex was my girlfriend, or wife, how could she be my wing-girl too?"

"Or your rescue when it all goes horribly wrong?" Lexie winked at him.

"Or the best friend I could ever wish for?" With his arm slung casually around the back of Lexie's chair, Callum leaned in and kissed her cheek.

"Urgh! You two are making the future Mr and Mrs Armstrong look only slightly keen on each other." Another friend arrived, and joined their growing reunion.

Lexie laughed and sipped her wine, hiding the blush she could feel rising in her cheeks. They all knew that more than likely before he'd even finished his first pint, Callum would be sizing up the single women in the room, and then she might not see him until it was time to head home in their shared taxi. That was one thing that hadn't changed since their student days. The man was incorrigible, charming, handsome, and (most devastatingly of all) entirely aware of the effect he had on probably 75% of the female population. Yes, those hazel eyes, currently glinting with mischief at her, could become dangerously smouldering when he wanted them to. She'd seen him disarm the most terrifying of no-nonsense women through a combination of one of his infamously-seductive stares, a casual tussle of his just-slightly-boyishly-long dark brown hair, and the half-grin for which he was notorious. That grin was currently targeted at her, as he raised his eyebrows in mock offence at her. Lexie had never seen Callum in action in the board-room, but could well imagine him being almost invincible when he needed to be. There was a reason he had risen to the top so swiftly. Charm and good looks were a dangerous combination in recruitment; how could anyone ever turn him down?

Sure enough, her prediction of his plans for the evening was correct.

"Lex, I'm going to go for a mingle. Save me a seat for when the buffet comes out?" With another kiss, he was gone, loosening his tie as he strolled away. She wondered why he even bothered tying it properly in the first place, given his tendency to remove it so soon after arriving anywhere.

"How do you put up with him, Lex?" asked Emily, Sam's girlfriend, moving into Callum's vacated seat and leaning in, conspiratorially, but with sympathy in her eyes.

"What's to put up with?" Lexie protested. "He's my best friend. And come on, you know how it is, how it's always been. We live three streets apart, and speak at least every other day – it's not like I need him in my pocket when we go out as well. Let him enjoy his mingling."

Emily sighed. "You're still doing the whole 'just friends' thing, then? Oh, come on; you're perfect together. You always have been. Surely you can see why we're always going on about it?"

"It isn't that simple," Lexie muttered, returning to her wine, and glad of the sudden in-crease in noise as the DJ started up in the corner. She glanced across the room to where Callum was already deep in conversation with the sister of the bride – the poor woman clearly hanging on his every word – and shook her head; there really was every chance Lexie would be getting the taxi home alone, despite their plans. Emily, like everyone else, was barking up the wrong tree. She and Cal were friends. She loved him, but not in that way, not any more, not after all this time. That's just the way it was. Why ruin a good thing?

Callum

The dancefloor in the centre of the ballroom was starting to fill up, as drinks flowed, loosening inhibitions, and music summoned a nostalgic vibe to the evening. Callum smiled as Lexie and the girls from their table abandoned handbags to the care of the remaining gents, now deep in conversation themselves, and headed to the floor, arms raised in excitement at the intro to a nineties 'classic'. He always loved the carefree version of Lexie that could be conjured up by a dose of nostalgia from their student days. It was a version that wasn't always around, far too often buried beneath the pressures of work or worrying about other people. Not tonight, he was glad to see. They really did need to get together with their university friends more often, if this was the result. The same had happened at his thirtieth, as they had played almost exactly the same music, and she had danced with the same group of girls, plus her best friends from work.

He paused for a moment as the bride's sister was distracted, swept into a hug by someone who Callum presumed was an uncle. Ever keen to keep Lexie happy, he set a reminder on his phone to bring up the subject the next day, not even pausing for a moment to consider whether he'd be seeing her. It was Sunday, so of course he would be seeing her. That was how things worked. Nothing was planned, it would just 'happen' once they were both up and about.

Twenty minutes later, having kept one eye on the dancefloor, Callum could see something was wrong.

Even from across the room, as he gave as much attention as he could spare to the Chief Bridesmaid-to-be, he could see a shadow darkening Lexie's previously-bright face. A man Callum didn't recognise was trying to separate Lexie from the rest of the girls, keeping himself in her eye-line, as much as she was making it obvious she had no interest in his attentions. This wouldn't do.

Callum didn't hesitate. Lexie might be one of the most independent woman he knew, but being independent didn't mean a bit of help wouldn't come in handy now and then.

Abandoning his drink, and making his apologies, Callum made his way through the crowd, not once taking his eyes off Lexie, wanting to be absolutely sure of her thoughts before wading in. She was looking even more uncomfortable now, still trying to dance her way away, but the guy, whoever he was, was being persistent. In that moment, Callum wished his friend wasn't always quite so stubborn, risking messing up her evening to prove the point that she was out to enjoy herself, but then, that's what he admired about her.

As he drew near her side, Callum reached out his hand, the slightest of touches to Lexie's, just so she would know he was there. If Lexie wanted to ignore him, that was her choice, but if she was after his help, she would know exactly where he was. Her fingers entwining with his was the sign he had been hoping for, as she glanced up at him, her eyes wide in a silent request for help. In one smooth movement, almost balletic, Callum spun Lexie into his arms, gripping her tightly around her waist, whilst she reached up around his neck, the two moving in time to the music, naturally in-sync as always.

"I was wondering where you were, sweetheart," he said, directly to Lexie, but loud enough that her unwelcome suitor would hear it. "Everything all right?" This last, he all but breathed into her ear, keeping up an appearance of romance between them.

She pulled back to look him in the face, her brightest smile lighting up her face. "All the better now you're back with me," she replied, also loud enough to be overheard.

Callum grinned back at her, pleased to see his favourite version of Lexie back, and happy that it was him who had achieved it.

Her admirer, seeing himself beaten, disappeared into the crowd, as Callum kept his grip on Lexie's waist; it would be good to keep the pretence up for a couple of more minutes, to make sure the guy got the message. Besides, the music wasn't that bad, and he could already see the buffet being brought out, so they'd all be heading back to their table soon enough anyway.

"Sorry I distracted you," Lexie leaned in again, and whispered in his ear, as the music changed, and they stayed put, swaying together in perfect harmony. "I think you've lost your bridesmaid."

"Ah, it's all right. I suspect, if I'm honest, she has half an eye on the best man," Callum replied, glancing back to where he had already been replaced. "Although, I see my glass has been cleared away already, so you do owe me a replacement."

Lexie laughed and clung onto him even tighter. "Fine.

Give it a few more minutes, then you grab us two plates of dinner, and I'll refresh our drinks. I'll get my bag."

When the next song ended, they finally separated, their fingers staying linked as they walked away from each other, until Callum noticed the smirks on the faces of Sam and Emily, already sitting at the group's table, plates loaded, and watching him and Lexie. He didn't let go any quicker than he would have done if he hadn't seen them. Let them watch, he thought; there was the same to see as usual: nothing. Two friends who kept an eye out for each other, and that was all there was to it. He and Lexie would laugh about it the next day, as they did every time anyone ever suggested they were anything more than friends.

SATURDAY 12TH OCTOBER

Lexie

It had been a tough week in the office. Having your dream job didn't mean there was no such thing as a bad day, and through a combination of clashing deadlines, ill colleagues and internal politics, she'd just had five of them in a row. Now, having enjoyed a rare lie-in, and spent a lazy day at home working through her list of chores, Lexie finally sank into the squidgy comfort of her sofa, and reached for the remote control. There had to be something on television to keep her entertained for a couple of hours before she headed for a long soak in the bath and an early night. She chuckled to herself at how rock-and-roll her life had become. Only just about to turn thirty, and she was as excited at the prospect of a quiet night in as she had been for the engagement party the weekend before.

At the other end of the sofa, her phone beeped, alerting her to a new message.

Callum: *Hey, up to much tonight?* x

She smiled at the sight of his name, then immediately tapped out a reply: *Huge plans… Bath and a book. You?* x

For half a moment, she wondered whether he had managed to find his way back into the bridesmaid's affections after he had come to her rescue at the Armstrongs' party, possibly even using the tale of his heroism to show off. She didn't have to wonder for long what else he might be up to, as her phone beeped again: *Date night – friend of T. Until usual x*

Lexie shook her head. One day that boy would end up in more trouble than he could handle. Tamsin was one of her closest friends at the newspaper where they both worked, and the two of them, plus their colleague Beth, were inseparable during the working week. Tamsin and Callum's brief fling the year before had somehow ending amicably, but the relationship had stirred strong emotions in the girls at work, ranging from admiration to jealousy, and even some mis-placed pity aimed in Lexie's direction when they discovered Callum was seeing one of her own friends. Somehow, the trio of girls had become closer friends when it all ended. But dating one of Tamsin's friends, if that's what it turned into? That had the potential to damage things at a wider level, and was not something Lexie wanted to be dealing with. The fall-out, she was sure, would no doubt start on Monday, but that was next week's problem, not one for tonight. 'Until usual' from Callum could mean anything – she would see him when she would see him, no doubt when he turned up at her flat the next morning – always his tendency on a Sunday, whether he had been out the night before or not.

He had his own key, the pair of them having swapped due to her tendency to worry when she went away anywhere, and his fear of losing the set to his own home; he could let himself in as long as she left the chain off. Lexie wondered if whether, for a change, she should stroll around to Callum's own flat, but having walked in on him and a date once before, that was not an experience she felt keen to repeat. She shuddered at the memory of finding the poor girl wrapped in one of Callum's sheets, trying to figure out how to use his coffee machine. In the end, with Callum nowhere to be found, Lexie had sorted it for her, and spent an uncomfortable quarter of an hour making small talk until the man himself had wandered in, still soaked from his shower. By then, luckily, Lexie had come up with a reasonable excuse for having needed to see him, handed him a random membership card from her purse, and hurried home. No, she definitely didn't need to do that again. He could come to her.

Bored of her unsuccessful scrolling through the channels, Lexie gave up, and headed through to run her bath.

Callum

Callum pocketed his phone and returned his attention to the bar, enjoying the buzz of the place, waiting for his drinks to be ready. There was always something mesmerising about watching cocktails being made, and he was on a date, after all; why not push the boat out and go for something more exotic than his usual Merlot or pint? He looked across the room to where Jess was sitting, smiling back at him. It was a good sign, the fact that she hadn't instantly reached for her phone the moment he left the table. Like he just had, and to send a message to another girl at that, he realised. He really shouldn't be asking Lexie what sort of evening she was having when he was out on a date with somebody else. Besides, he had a feeling he was in for a good night if he played his cards right. Texting other women was not playing his cards right. Collecting the cocktails, he nodded his thanks, and returned to his date.

It didn't take Callum long to make his excuses and leave Jess' flat the next morning. A surprise Sunday morning meeting with a possible new client was always easy to fake, and impossible for anyone to disprove, even if they wanted to. Jess hadn't, accepting his excuse without question, and reminding him of her availability the next weekend. There was a flicker of guilt in Callum's heart for a moment when he realised that not only was he busy the next Saturday, he also wasn't too troubled to see her again. With a final kiss on the cheek, he headed out of the door. For mid-October, it was a bright, sunny morning, and he decided to make the most of it, having been cooped up in the office all week, walking home rather than hopping on the Tube. An hour or so of fresh air would do him the world of good, especially with so few people about at that time of day.

Once he had showered and changed, a quick glance at the clock told him that knowing Lexie, she'd also be up and about by now, and hopefully in the mood for a coffee and a chat. After all, he hadn't seen her other than to wave from a train window in the last week. There would be plenty to catch up on.

Grabbing his jacket, he checked his pockets, and headed out of the door.

"Lex? You up? I'll make coffee!" He called his greeting into the flat as he opened her front door, pleased to hear music playing in the living room. She was up, then.

"I wondered if you might be coming over," she called back from the kitchen, as Callum shrugged off his jacket and hung it on the rail by the door. "I'm making pancakes. Want some?"

Callum grinned. He had definitely made the right decision to leave Jess' place and head around here instead. "What can I do?" he asked, as he hugged her from behind, planting a kiss on the back of her head.

"Get the coffee on; I ground the beans, but didn't get any further." She wriggled out of his arms, but not before Callum squeezed her tight again.

Without another word, they became a seamless machine: Lexie at the hob, Callum pottering around the rest of the kitchen, gathering mugs and milk and preparing their coffees. Just like almost every Sunday. It was as domestic as he was ever going to get, thought Callum, not altogether upset at the fact. He and Lexie always fell into the most natural of rhythms when it was just the two of them, one he certainly never felt inclined to with anyone else.

"How was your date?" she finally asked, as she put two plates out on the immaculately-clean worktop, ready for the pancakes.

How had it been? All right, he figured. "It was… fine." He paused for a moment. "Yeah, it was fine. Went to that new bar I told you about, in Piccadilly. Thought I could try it out."

"Worth going back to?"

"Yes, but not with Jess. Maybe we could give it a go one weekend?"

"More than happy to. Not seeing her again then?"

Callum shook his head, then realised Lexie wasn't looking at him. "No. She's a nice girl, but, I don't know. Didn't click." He'd not let on that despite not clicking, he had still ended up back at her place. No doubt Lexie could work that out for herself, if she even cared. He wondered for a moment whether she did.

"Sorry to hear it. Still, Beth will be pleased. You should have seen the daggers she was firing at Tams on Wednesday when she twigged that Tams had sent you Jess' number."

"I'm pleased I'm still such a source of envy and gossip at your office."

"You need to watch it though, Cal. It's a fine line between being a romantic rogue and the cad who loves us and leaves us. Make sure you stay on the right side of it." For a moment, Lexie stopped what she was doing, turned, and looked straight at him, her hands on his chest. "I mean it, you know? Be the good guy, who we roll our eyes at but still adore, not the bastard we hate ourselves for even thinking about getting involved with."

It was nowhere near as bad as what others had called him in the past, but Lexie's words hit home. He trod a treacherous path at times, seeing girls he knew were friends-of-friends for Lexie. Any hurt could hit a little too close to home if he wasn't careful. He took Lexie's hands in his, pulling them closer together.

"I'll watch it, I promise. And anyway, we're getting to that time of year, aren't we? Way too many nights out in the diary already, so no time to fit in any more poorly-thought-out dates." Seeing Lexie wasn't entirely reassured, Callum grinned, then leaned over and kissed her forehead. "It will be fine, I promise." And Callum didn't break promises to Lexie.

SATURDAY 19TH OCTOBER

Lexie

The club was heaving, but Lexie was, for once, enjoying the noise and the crowd. Dancing with the girls from work didn't happen often these days, but when they put their minds to it, they all embraced their inner teen, finding the place playing the cheesiest pop classics from their student days. They may not have studied together, but the spirit was the same. And tonight, the girls had gone out with one goal, and one goal alone: a classic Girls' Night Out. No men, that was tonight's rule. Tams had even got them a comfy booth for the night, a perk of having reviewed a couple of gigs for the club the month before. Life was good.

As a bottle of Prosecco appeared out of nowhere on the table in front of them, Lexie realised that, as always, the 'no men' rule really meant 'no men other than Callum'. It was true that she hadn't expected to see him that night, but rather than annoyance, a smile spread across her face. She ignored the jocular glares from some of the girls, and grinned up at him.

"Ladies," he called to the rest of the table. "Don't worry, I know this is your night, but I wanted to give Mark

14

a 'Welcome to London' party, and Tams said she could get us in here. We won't disturb you, but get Lex to text me, and there'll be another one of these whenever you want it. As many as you like. All on me." Tapping the top of the bottle, Callum winked at her, and headed back across the club to the bar, where a man was standing, two pints in front of him on the tall table.

"Who's Mark?" asked Beth, her eyes following Callum's route through the crowd.

"Old schoolfriend. They go way back." Lex started to pour the Prosecco into their waiting glasses as she answered.

"Further back than you? Must be a rarity," chipped in Tams.

Lexie smirked back at them, as the others re-joined the table, clapping their hands at the arrival of the bottle. "Since they were five or six, I think. He's a good guy, from what I've heard. Been out of the country for years though; only just moved back."

"He's cute too, assuming this is him," observed Beth, nodding her head.

Lexie looked over. Sure enough, the man who had been waiting for Callum was now approaching the table himself, clutching another bottle of fizz. At this rate, there were going to be hangovers all round in the morning. Putting down the bottle she had been pouring from, Lexie rose to meet him and was immediately swept into a huge bear-hug as though they were long-lost friends. Yes, Beth was right, she mused, Mark certainly was cute. Whilst Lexie had to admit Callum had the classic 'tall, dark and handsome' sexiness about him, Mark was more boyish in appearance, a 'blond hair blue eyes' combination which had always drawn her in during her younger years.

"You must be Lexie; Cal described you to perfection," he said, releasing her from the hug, and reaching for her hand, raising it to his lips.

"And you must be Mark – I've heard a lot about you."

15

She was at risk of blushing like a teenager, Lexie thought, retrieving her hand and smoothing non-existent creases from her dress.

"Likewise. And all good, I swear." He smiled at her, his eyes practically shining. "I hope we can get to know each other properly, perhaps over a quiet drink sometime?"

Lexie felt the eyes of the table on her. "I don't see that being a problem," she replied, carefully not looking over to where Callum would be standing. "But tonight is girls' night, as well you should know, so you can leave that bottle, and be on your way."

Mark swept them all a ridiculous bow, and headed back to the other side of the bar where Callum was waiting.

"You're never going to go out with him?" Tamsin demanded, reaching for Callum's bottle to finish topping up their glasses.

Lexie was still watching Mark's retreating back. In truth, she wasn't sure whether she would or wouldn't take Mark up on his offer, but it was certainly nice to be asked. After all, she hadn't been out on a date for months. It wasn't the most fun, always being the one sitting at home, knowing your best friend was out on a date that he would no doubt tell you all about the next day. Besides, being taken out by somebody else would certainly give Callum something to think about.

Wait. Where had that idea come from?

"If you take Mark, does that mean Callum's on the market?"

Beth's question jolted Lexie from what felt like worrying thoughts. "What's Cal's relationship status got to do with me going out, or not, with Mark?"

"Oh, come on," Beth scoffed. "Surely it's just a matter of time for you two?"

There it was again. Everyone's assumption that she and Callum were simply killing time until they got together. "If it was a matter of time, why would I be planning to go out with his best friend?" Suddenly, it seemed a good idea. If

Mark did ask, she would say yes. It would probably do her good. If nothing else, it would stop everyone asking when she and Callum were going to become a couple. "Anyway, come on, we said no men tonight, and that means no talking about them either." She picked up her glass and took a long swig. "They can buy us drinks and be gone. Pretty much the perfect contribution to the evening in my book."

Callum

From across the bar, Callum had watched the interaction between Lexie and Mark with a strange mixture of curiosity and confusion. It would be good if his two best friends began dating each other, wouldn't it? They could form a happy little trio, all hanging out, having a laugh, enjoying life. But however hard he tried, somehow it didn't sit right.

"She's a lovely girl, your Lexie," said Mark, returning to his stool. "Gorgeous friends too."

Callum nodded. "I think Beth fancies me."

"Probably. You won't go out with her though."

"Why not? I've dated Lex's friends before. Although, around that table, only Tams. It's never been a problem in the past, hence we are here tonight, free of charge, and discounts on drinks."

Mark smirked. "All right. Here's a question for you. Do you, or do you not, think Lexie is attractive?"

The question made Callum pause, pint halfway to his mouth. How on earth did he answer this one? "Well, I've never really thought about it."

"Come on, you must have, or you wouldn't be human. And it's an easy enough question. Yes or no. Do you think Lexie is attractive?"

"All right, I would have to say, yes, she is attractive." He paused. "I mean of course she is; she's gorgeous." There was no point lying about what was plainly obvious to anyone with eyes.

"I don't think you mean it."

"What? How can you know who I do or don't find attractive? And why push me for an answer, if you're not going to believe me when I give it?"

"Because," replied Mark, "every woman you've ever expressed any serious interest in, that you've ever told me about, is the polar opposite of Lexie in one way or another. Look at her, properly I mean, and think about the last, what, five women you've dated, for any length of time, and tell me I'm not right. Even the ones I've seen you checking out tonight fit the bill. It had been niggling me whenever we talked, or I saw photos of the pair of you, but now I've met her in person, it's so obvious."

Callum looked around the bar. It was true; he'd noticed a few girls as they'd walked in, and had even caught the eye of a couple, working out whether he might stand a chance. Mostly blondes or redheads, nothing like the brunette Lexie, and completely different in style, even the way they carried themselves. "Coincidence, that's all it is. Coincidence." Of course it was.

"Yeah, course it is." Mark raised his eyebrows as he drank the end of his pint.

Wasn't it? Movement across the club caught his eye, as Lexie and the girls left their booth and headed to the dancefloor as one. Callum laughed at the song that had got them to their feet – a Europop 'classic', Lexie would always claim, whenever she requested it, which she must have done tonight – but he couldn't help, just for a moment, wishing he could be up there with them. With them, or with her? No, with them, definitely. The club was filling up, and the atmosphere building. He and Mark would have a few more drinks, and then see where the night took them.

Lexie

As the music, and alcohol, surged through her, Lexie felt the stresses of the week drift further away with each and every song. Almost without realising it, her gaze flicked back to Callum and Mark every few minutes, until the floor filled to the extent she could no longer see through the mass of bodies. It was for the best, she thought, angry with herself for being so distracted on what was meant to be a chance for them all to let their hair down.

As the crowds parted, she realised the reason she couldn't see them any more was the simple fact that they had gone; the tall stools they had been perched on were empty now, about to be moved out of the way, to make more room around the dancefloor now the night was progressing. The boys must have moved on. A good thing, in the grand scheme of the evening.

Or so Lexie thought, until Beth made a grab for her hand. Thinking her friend just wanted another drink, or to pull her further into the mass of bodies that was surrounding them, Lexie turned, smiling, until the concerned look on Beth's face gave her pause. Following her line of sight, there was Callum, just feet away from them, dancing with, or rather being heavily leaned against, by a leggy blonde, who looked decidedly worse for wear. For once in his life, he didn't look delighted to be the centre of a woman's attention.

"I think he needs rescuing," shouted Beth, above the din. "Do you mind if I step in?"

Actually, Lexie found that she did mind, fractionally, but in that moment, there was no point saying anything. Beth was closer, and clearly intent on being Callum's saviour. Lexie nodded, stepping aside as Beth adjusted her top and headed towards Callum.

Amidst the crowds, Beth danced her way across to Callum as naturally as she could, until she found herself next to her target. Lexie watched as she somehow managed to step between Callum and his new-found 'friend', smiling at the reaction on his face; an odd combination of initial confusion, swiftly replaced by obvious relief. Just as he had done with Lexie the previous week, Callum eased his arm around Beth's waist as they both made some attempt at apologetic smiles to the blonde.

They looked good together, Lexie had to admit. The blonde gave up and staggered unsteadily away, as Callum smiled down at Beth, now leaning into him as he shouted something into her ear, causing her to tilt her head back and laugh. Was this how others saw her and Callum, Lexie wondered, an odd sense of regret tugging somewhere deep inside. Should she have stepped in, rather than Beth? Callum didn't seem to mind, she thought, as they remained deep in conversation, not bothering to keep up any pretence of dancing.

Shaking her head to try and clear her mind, Lexie turned back to the rest of the girls, and kept dancing. No doubt she would get Callum's full thoughts on the matter soon enough.

SATURDAY 26TH OCTOBER

Lexie

In her bag, Lexie's phone buzzed into life. Ignoring it, she focused on the conversation going on around her. It was still early, and the local pub she and the girls had headed to still was fairly quiet, both in terms of people and volume.

"He never did!"

Lexie turned. She'd clearly missed something in the discussion, despite the lack of distractions. "Who never did what, Beth?"

"Pete actually asked me to cover something other than a WAG getting a manicure. It's a miracle."

Lexie grinned, genuinely happy for her friend, and joined in the clink of champagne flutes. It was extravagant, but who cared? You only had one birthday a year, and she was determined to celebrate. Girls tonight, and something with Callum tomorrow. Probably. Although strictly speaking nothing had been arranged yet. He would be in touch come the morning, she suspected.

Her phone buzzed again. Sighing, she dipped into her bag and retrieved it. Callum. She grinned; here came her plans for the next day. Waving an apology to the girls, she clicked to answer, turning away from the conversation to hear what he wanted.

"Hey you, what's up?"

"Where are you?"

"Not even a 'Hello'? Rude. I'm out, in the Hart, with the girls. As you would have known if you had actually listened when you asked what I was up to this weekend."

A pause. "What are you wearing?"

Lexie laughed. "What sort of question is that?"

"A genuine one. What are you wearing?"

"Black cocktail dress, silver heels. We're going on somewhere smart later, apparently." Although the girls hadn't actually told her where yet.

"The black one with the lace sleeves?"

It really couldn't be a good sign that he knew her wardrobe so intimately. "That's the one."

"Excellent, you'll do. Fancy dinner at The Citizen?"

"The Citizen?"

"Please? I may have been stood up, but that's no reason to give up the reservation – you know how long their waiting list is."

Lexie sighed, not realising she had done it out loud.

"Oh, come on, it's one of the finest restaurants in town, not some trashy burger van. You could sound at least a little bit happier about the prospect?"

"All right, fine, you're right, it is too good an opportunity to miss. When do you want me there?"

"Eight?"

She glanced at her watch. Forty minutes. It was doable if she left now. "I'll be there."

As she hung up, the girls were looking on, expectantly.

"A date?" Beth asked.

"Cal," Lexie replied. "And The Citizen. So, I am sorry, ladies, but coffee somewhere tomorrow instead?"

"As long as you don't expect us to stop partying because you are?"

Laughing, Lexie hugged them each in turn, finished her drink, and headed for the door.

She made it with five minutes to spare, seeing Cal waiting outside. Whoever it was who had stood him up had clearly missed a trick. Even from a distance, she could see he was wearing the new designer jacket he had been raving about the week before, and his smartest indigo-blue jeans, with the collar of his dark blue shirt opened just enough at the neck, his tie just casually enough loosened; he certainly knew what he was doing when he got ready for an evening... It must have been somebody worthwhile for that level of effort. He was intently staring at his phone as she crept up behind him, covering his eyes with her hands.

"Lex!" He pulled her hands away and turned to look at her. "Perfect."

She twirled, smiling at his compliment. "You've scrubbed up pretty well yourself. Shall we?"

The flowers arrived as their divine starters of chicken parfait and smoked salmon were cleared away. Purple freesias, in a beautiful bloom. Lexie's favourite flowers, in her favourite colour.

"As requested," the waiter said, placing them on the table with a flourish, smiling at Lexie.

"Flowers?" she asked teasingly. "And my favourites too… Who exactly was this girl, Cal?"

"Oh, they're your favourites, are they? I did wonder where I'd got the idea, even as I was ordering them."

She narrowed her eyes at him, but the arrival of their main courses prevented any further questioning, as she tucked into the perfectly-grilled pork chop, surrounded with fondant potato and apple slices. She was vaguely aware of the attention the flowers gesture had drawn to their table. Well, if the other diners were expecting a proposal, they were going to be sorely disappointed. Still, the food was good enough; diners shouldn't expect a show as well.

The gift-box arrived after desert. With champagne.

Decent champagne at that.

Lexie eyed Cal. "Do you want to take this back and use it another time? As much as I'm enjoying getting a dose of the full Callum Fitzpatrick Date Experience, honestly, Cal, she really must have been somebody special to go to this length for her."

"She was. She is." He gestured to the box. "Happy Birthday, Lexie."

For a moment, it was as though the air had been knocked out of her. "This? You? For me?"

He shrugged. That annoying, endearing shrug that he always believed would get him out of any trouble he found himself in. It usually did. Slowly, suddenly nervous, she pulled at the ribbon, opened the box, and laughed. A tiny plastic toad, definitely not a frog, held in resin, and on a delicate silver chain. Her favourite character, from her favourite cartoon series as a child.

"I love it," she whispered. "Thank you, Cal, this has been a lovely evening, truly, the best birthday celebration I could have asked for."

"Well, the night is still young. What would you say to a night-cap? Back at mine?"

"You know, you could have just told me straight that you wanted to take me out to dinner." Lexie kicked off her heels and sank into Cal's black leather sofa, accepting the glass of wine Cal handed her, and leaned back. His sofa, with its angles and metal legs, would never be as comfortable as hers, but it suited the rest of the flat. She still couldn't convince him to add cushions.

"You wouldn't have come. You'd have found some excuse, and palmed me off with coffee and cake tomorrow afternoon."

It was true, Lexie had to admit to herself, knowing what she had thought earlier that very evening. Despite all the dinners and parties they went to, a formal dinner date, just the two of them other than just grabbing a bite to eat at the pub, was a rarity. It all felt a little too formal, too fixed, somehow, going against the grain of their 'just friends' stance.

"Do you still want to do coffee and cake tomorrow?" Somehow, she knew the girls wouldn't mind having their plans rearranged, and had a feeling their heads wouldn't necessarily be in the best place for a wander in the park.

"Of course." Whisky in hand, he sat at the other end of the sofa, and reached for the remote.

Two clicks, and music began playing softly in the background, the soundtrack to their evening's continuing chatter.

Callum

Callum wasn't sure exactly when the night had started to feel dangerous. The flowers had been touch-and-go, but he'd bluffed his way through that easily enough. The gift had gone down well, and her laughter had broken any tension there, but now, with Lex lounging back on his sofa, her feet having found their way into his lap, he was no longer sure. Mark's words kept flitting through his mind – however far back he went in his memory, he had never dated anyone remotely similar to Lex. He hadn't even been drawn to anyone when on nights out with the lads, or away with work. Of course it wasn't a coincidence, however hard he had claimed that to his friend. It was self-defence. He had yo-yoed back and forth so much in his feelings for Lexie over the years, without saying a word to her or anyone else, that these days, he found the safest thing was to avoid her type entirely when he was unattached. He watched her flick through the music selection on his phone, her face serious until she came across something she liked, and hit *Play*. That was a rarity in itself, letting anyone else near his phone. Focusing, he considered her properly, objectively, for the first time in years. He didn't like the direction his mind had started wandering.

"I never took my spare clothes home in the end, did I?"

Her voice broke into his thoughts. Where the hell had that come from? Had he been so obviously ignoring her, lost in his own thoughts? "Um, no. No, you didn't." He pulled himself together. "My room, left-hand wardrobe, bottom shelf." A pair of jeans, a couple of tops, a pair of trainers and a small toiletry bag he had assumed held underwear and, well, toiletries, but he'd never opened it to find out. Why would he?

"Good."

"You're heading home then?" Strangely, the notion saddened him.

"At some point, I'll probably have to." Reaching out to put her wine glass on the coffee table, Lexie swung her legs off Callum's lap and rose to her feet.

The sofa already felt emptier, as Lexie wandered out of the room and headed towards his bedroom. It unsettled him for a moment, until he shook his head to clear his mind. Not sure why it was suddenly important, Callum went and refreshed both their drinks. If she returned to a full glass of wine, even in jeans and a t-shirt, she might feel inclined to stay a big longer before calling a cab and leaving him to his ever-more discomfiting thoughts.

"I have good news and bad news, Cal," she called from his bedroom, a few minutes later.

"Hit me?"

"The good news is that despite lying about being stood up, you are still going to have a beautiful woman in your bed tonight. The bad news," she popped her head around the door, "is that it's going to be me, and I've just stolen your best PJs."

She wasn't wrong. A heartbeat later, Lexie stepped fully into the living room and reclaimed her end of the sofa, looking expectantly at him, until he did the same, her feet once again finding their home in his lap. It took him longer than it should have done for him to stop staring at her, as she smiled, raising her glass in thanks for the top-up. It was troubling how naturally she fitted into the ridiculously oversized silk pyjamas his parents had bought him a couple of years ago. He had never worn them, preferring boxers and a t-shirt, if anything.

"It's late, and I can't be bothered to get a taxi home. Plus," she grinned, leaning back against the arm of the sofa. "Your bed's bigger than mine, even if it does hold the sordid imprints of your various conquests."

Callum laughed. The one secret between them, the one thing he had never revealed to her, and if he had his way, he never would. Despite everything, Lex was the only girl who had ever slept in his bed. Bringing others back to his had never been his way; it was much easier to stay at theirs. That way, he was in control. Staying over at his date's, he could decide whether the next morning required a long, leisurely breakfast at her house, a romantic brunch somewhere, or a quick getaway. No awkwardness waiting for her to finish using his bathroom, or wondering what exactly to offer her in terms of coffee or breakfast. He could be away, back to his friends. To his best friend. Even the lucky few who had risen to the esteemed but often short-lived position of 'girlfriend' didn't sleep at Callum's flat. Visited, yes, spent time in the bed, yes, but stayed over and slept there? Never.

"What about your clothes bag?"

"For the morning, of course. I refuse to let people think I'm doing the 'walk of shame', even if it is just for a couple of streets. Jeans and trainers make it far easier to blend into a crowd."

"I'm on my own sofa then? Thanks. And after I've bought you dinner and everything."

"Don't be daft. We've shared before, we can share again. But I'm not tired yet; I just wanted to get comfy." She took another sip of wine before continuing. "It was good to meet Mark last week. He's permanently here now?"

"Mark? Yeah."

"We should all get together. I think I like Mark."

So did Callum, but he didn't like the way the conversation was turning. Despite what she had just said, he was more tired than he had realised, and now very keen for an excuse for the current topic of conversation to end. "I'm done in, I think," he said, stretching, before seeing what would inevitably happen next. "Mind, I could be convinced to sit up for another, if you fancy?"

Lexie looked thoughtfully at her glass. "We'll sit up until we finish these, ok?"

He nodded, torn between downing the dregs of his whisky, and making what remained of the drink last as long as possible. In the end, he went for the latter, turning the conversation onto safer topics, such as work, and Christmas shopping.

Within the hour, they were both in his king-sized bed, with Callum glad he'd made the decision to change the sheets that very morning. Not that he wanted the moment to be romantic, but as Lexie snuggled under the covers next to him, he was pleased they were still smelling of fresh laundry liquid, making her smile at the scent.

"Sleep well, Lex, and kick me if you need anything in the night."

"With pleasure, Cal." She leaned over, and kissed him on the cheek before switching off the bedside lamp. "Goodnight."

Callum woke with his usual Sunday-morning hint of a hangover, combined with the dim feeling of contentedness. He shifted position, only to find his arm trapped. Trapped? A girl. He forced his eyes and brain to focus. His bed, his flat, so which… Oh. Lexie. During the night, the edges of their 'sides' had clearly blurred, and Lexie was now sound asleep, her head resting on his shoulder, his right arm under her body, hers over his. Entwined.

"Lex?" No reaction to his whisper. Seeing no way out of the situation without waking her, he leaned his head back against the pillow. He could have a lie-in. It was strange, in a way. Usually on a Sunday morning he'd be thinking about his plans with the very girl he had just woken up with. Did that mean they would still have plans, or that she would indeed stroll home, and not see him again until the next weekend? For some reason, he hoped it was the latter, uncertain what exactly what they would do if she stayed. He racked his brain to try and remember what they were doing the following Saturday, certain that 'something' was in his diary, but not a clue what. Lexie stirred beside him. "Hey, you awake?"

"No, definitely not," she mumbled, rolling away from him and burying her head deeper under the duvet.

"I'll get the coffee," he replied, ignoring her protests, and pulling the covers away in one swift movement, now he was free to do so. "Then you need to get in touch with the girls." Or do anything else, he thought, as long as it meant leaving his flat. He wasn't sure he could handle their usual pattern of domesticity in his own home.

SATURDAY 2ᴺᴰ NOVEMBER

Lexie

Party starts at 7. Get here for 6.15, and I'll book the taxi for 6.30? x

It was a simple enough message, thought Lexie, as she typed it out and hit Send. Things had been stilted between her and Callum for the last week, with only the briefest of strolls through Richmond Park to see the deer after work on her actual birthday, but surely, everything was fine by now? Especially as she didn't even truly understand why things were so awkward. His treat had been special, true enough, but nothing untoward had happened. On the Sunday morning they had chatted over coffee, then she had headed back to hers before meeting the girls in the park. Exactly how she had expected the day to go, having abandoned them the night before. And yet, Cal had almost seemed relieved to see her go, as she headed out of his door mid-morning. Not at all the way he usually acted around her, and even stranger when she considered how often they spent all day together on a Sunday, with not a hint of awkwardness.

Her phone buzzed with an almost instant response: *Sorry, can't make it. Hope you have a good evening. C x*

Not the response she was expecting. "Callum!" Taking her moment of anger out on an un-fortunate throw-cushion, she hit *Dial*; he wasn't going to be let off the hook that easily. "What are you playing at, Cal? You promised." She hardly gave him chance to draw breath as he answered.

He did at least have the decency to sound genuinely apologetic. "I'm sorry, Lex, truly I am, but something's come up."

"This has been in your diary for *months*. I even reminded you on Wednesday, and you said you were still coming."

"I know, but, well, like I say, something's come up. And besides, you said yourself, it's just your usual colleagues. It's not like one of my client events. Everyone at your office knows we're just friends; it isn't such a big deal."

"What?" Of all the things Lexie had thought he might say, that wasn't it. "It's not about that, and you know it."

"Of course it is. At my things, you pretend to be my girlfriend, and at yours, I pretend to be your boyfriend. Isn't it getting just a bit, well, obvious? Pretty sure everyone at your place is wise to it by now. They'll be laughing at us, it's so blatant. It's pointless."

"But—"

"Look, I'm sorry, I am, but there's nothing to be done. Like I say, hope you have a good time, and I'll catch you soon."

Without giving her a chance to respond, Callum had hung up, leaving Lexie staring at her phone. Well, she wasn't going to stand for that, she thought, hitting *Redial*. "Are you implying my work events aren't as important as yours?" she demanded, continuing their conversation as though it hadn't even been paused.

"All right, if you're going to start putting words in my mouth, yes, at times, I do," Callum replied. "At least the events we go to with my colleagues are with different clients, different projects. At the paper, it's always the same crowd, year-in, year-out. It's all a bit daft, surely?"

"I… I just—"

"I've got to go, sorry." Again, Callum ended the call, leaving Lexie speechless, and without the energy to call a third time.

She dropped onto the sofa, any inclination to attempt to impress her boss gone out of the window. How could Callum do this to her? Tonight would have been the first 'do' of the party season, as they began the rush towards Christmas. Her outfit had been planned, and everything sorted. Despite her fury, Lexie ran her fingers over the jewellery box in front of her on the coffee table, the toad set in resin sitting happily inside. It didn't go at all with her outfit (in all fairness, what outfit would it go with? – it was a plastic toad!), but Lexie had had every intention of wearing it that night, to show Callum what she thought of his gift and how much it meant to her. A small gesture, but one she was sure he would have appreciated. It shouldn't have mattered, but suddenly, wearing it was the last thing she planned to do. She didn't want to think about Callum Fitzpatrick at all.

Callum

For a good twenty minutes, all Callum could do was stare at his phone, and think about what an idiot he was being. Not to mention an appalling friend. But could he really turn up at Lexie's office party and pretend everything was normal, after what had happened the weekend before? His head was a mess, thinking and over-thinking about what Mark had said, and the way everything had felt so comfortable the previous Sunday. He hated lying to Lexie, and he hated letting her down, but in that moment, it felt better than the alternative.

It was only as he watched the hours tick by that he realised that the next weekend was his own company's own post-Bonfire Night party, which Lexie was due to attend at his side. All too late, he could only imagine the amount of grovelling he was going to have to do if he was going to stand a chance of her being there. Perhaps, if he just went to her party, that would make things easier? He could go, stand, chat nicely with Beth, Tams and the others, no problem at all. Except, he couldn't. Not now.

He didn't even know what was going on in his own mind. All he could picture whenever he let his mind drift was Lexie lying there, wrapped in his bedding, looking a picture of tranquillity. For the first time in years, they had both been single, and for a good few months now, at the same time. He was lonely. Or she was. Or they both were. That was it. They had shared beds on weekends away, at nights crashed in friends' homes, all sorts, with no problems before. It was just boredom. Nothing to worry about. Nothing he should be worrying about as much as this.

But as he poured himself a whisky, and his mind was once again on his upcoming party, all he could do was wonder how the hell he was going to get out of this one…

Lexie

Lexie could feel the sympathy in Beth and Tamsin's looks as she worked her way through the third glass of champagne she had accepted, almost without thinking, from the passing tray. She wasn't sure what she was angrier about: Callum letting her down, or how hurt she felt at his decision. Despite trying so hard to focus on what was going on around her, all she could do was play and over-play the weekend before. Their surprise dinner at The Citizen had been wonderful, and although there had been a couple of odd moments, like the flowers, everything had been so positive. But then, Sunday morning had come, and she could sense Callum's almost desperation for her to be up and out of his flat. It made no sense; they had spent so many Sunday mornings together in the past, so what had been different this time? She had even spent the night at his before, chatting away, staying over, sharing his bed… There was nothing different, was there?

Except, there was. Something in the whirlwind of their semi-date had changed things, even if she couldn't immediately put her finger on it. Lexie thought back to all the little moments that had happened recently, from Callum referencing her specifically at his birthday party, their dance at the engagement party, the flicker of envy as he danced with Beth in the club, to the comfort of waking up in his arms last weekend. Things were changing, and she didn't know what to think about it.

She should have stayed and made him talk to her; Lexie could see that now. But she had been in a state of, what, shock? Certainly surprise. Not even coffee and cake with the girls had helped soothe her mind.

Before she knew what was happening, Beth was pressing a fourth glass of fizz into her hand and whisking her away into a flurry of conversation. Lexie had to think, that was certain, but it wasn't going to be done this evening.

SATURDAY 9TH NOVEMBER

Lexie

"Please? Come on, Lexie. I'll do anything. I know I let you down, badly, but please – you know this one is important." The desperation in Callum's voice was clear.

"Just as it was important for me last week, Cal. You're not the only one who has people you're keen to impress." Lexie closed her eyes and leaned back on her sofa, unsure for a moment who she was more upset with: Callum, for letting her down last weekend, or herself, for the fact that she was clearly about to forgive him. She had missed him the weekend before, although she would never have admitted it to the girls.

"Have I told you recently that you're the most amazing person I know? Can I come around? There's some stuff I need to run through before the party." He was already so confident he was going to get his way.

Lexie sighed. At the end of the day, she knew she was giving in, and might as well accept it. And, pathetic as it was, she wanted to see him. "Fine. I'm in all day, come around whenever you like."

She had hardly had chance to hang up on him when the doorbell rang. Lexie tutted; if it wasn't one thing, it was another. She pulled open the door.

"Cal?"

"The one and only." He spread his arms wide, a hopeful smile on his face, but the bags under his eyes betrayed that perhaps he had been sleeping as badly as Lexie for the last two weeks.

"Were you out here the whole time? Why did you even ring?"

"I wasn't convinced you'd forgive me over the phone, or at all, so I figured I'd come over, just in case, to make sure I could do all I could to persuade you that I'm sorry, and that I won't ever do anything so stupid or callous again. And besides, you did just tell me you were in all day." He paused for a moment and shook his head. "I needed to see you."

Gritting her teeth to stop herself smiling at his last words, Lexie stepped back and let him in, noticing the suit carriers draped over his arm. "Are you planning on being here until the party?"

He shrugged. "Seemed sensible, if you gave me that option."

"You were so confident I'd forgive you, one way or another?"

As he dropped his carriers over the back of the sofa, Callum revealed a box of her favourite chocolates, and grinned at her. "I was an absolute idiot, Lex. I let you down, badly, and I don't even have a good reason for it. But I'm a hopeful idiot, and also your own personal idiot, whether you like it or not." He went to hand her the box. "Thank you for saying you'll come tonight. I really appreciate it, especially as I know I don't deserve it. Don't deserve you. Because, you see, there's something else."

Lexie narrowed her eyes at him. "Go on? I'm not accepting these until I know what I'm agreeing to."

"A Mr and Mrs Competition," he said, a glimmer of a smile in his eyes. "Come on, it'll be fun?" he continued, hope clear in his voice.

"Oh no, Cal. Why?" Lexie wasn't even going to try and disguise the exasperation in her voice.

He took a deep breath, and looked her straight in the eye. "I'm sorry. Again. They wanted anyone signed up as bringing a partner to take part, and bring a little light entertainment to the evening so it wasn't just everyone sitting around talking and drinking. And there's a decent prize at the end of it, for the winners. I reckon we have a good chance, looking at some of the couples who've signed up."

"People do know we aren't an actual couple, don't they? I mean, your close colleagues, if not the clients?"

Callum turned away and headed into the kitchen.

"Callum?"

"It's a grey area," he called over his shoulder.

"What!" She sank into her chair. "No," she said, as he waved a bottle of wine at her, eyebrows raised in question. "If I'm entering a quiz, then I'm keeping a clear head, and so are you."

"Fine," he replied, returning the bottle to the fridge. "Coffee it is then."

As Callum bustled around in the kitchen, Lexie dropped her head into her hands. She really did let him get away with too much, she thought. Once again, he had let her down, driven her almost to distraction, and then swept in with his charm in time to win her back over. The man would make a terrible boyfriend; probably the reason he never seemed to be one for any noticeable length of time. She looked across to the suit bags, wondering what options Callum had brought, and what she'd be best wearing to align with him. The annual post-Bonfire Night do was always a big deal; it was critical they looked their best if the hosts were to think she and Callum were a couple. Needing to be doing 'something' in order to keep herself focused, Lexie stood up and headed through to her spare bedroom, affectionately known as her walk-in wardrobe, where she kept her smarter outfit options.

Callum wasn't far behind her, two full mugs in his hands. "Ah, the room where the magic happens. I was going to go with the suit I wore to the Armstrong do; what do you reckon?"

"Good choice." He had looked smart that night. "Tie?"

"Burgundy?"

Lexie nodded, skimmed through the rail of her long wardrobe, and pulled out two dresses. "Long or short?"

"Short."

Short it was then. "I always feel a bit like a cheerleader in this one, until I glam it up with the accessories." Even before she glammed it up, the black skater-style dress was one of her favourites, with a navy and burgundy floral pattern starting lightly, then building on the skirt. Long enough to look good for a classy event, but short enough to still be youthful and fun. Black tights and her trusty silver heels, and she'd be good to go. She gave it a quick shake, and hung it up on the back of the door, all set for when she got ready later.

"I think we've done this in record time," said Callum, sitting at the head of her spare bed, having shifted the cushions to one side.

"You needn't have bothered coming around so early," Lexie replied, leaning against the chest of drawers opposite him. "What will we do for," she glanced at her watch, "six hours, until we need to get in the taxi, which I am assuming you've already booked?"

"I have, and four hours, surely, building in time for a couple of showers, perfecting that 'glamour power couple' look we'll be going for."

"I know what we need to do." She pulled out her phone. "Practise our Mr and Mrs responses, if you want the prize so much."

"Do we have to?"

"It's either that, or you actually explain what the hell was going on with you last weekend. I've forgiven you, just, and I will come tonight, but it hurt, Cal, and especially after such a good time the Saturday before. It didn't make sense."

Callum

It didn't make sense, not even to himself, however many times he had relived the experience in his mind. Of course, he and Lexie had had their fair share of disagreements in their fifteen years of friendship, or they wouldn't be human, but he'd never intentionally started one before. And it wasn't as though he hadn't wanted to be there for her and support her. But after their evening out for her birthday, and thinking about what Mark had said, the thought of being in her company had all just felt a bit too much. How could he possibly tell her that? He forced himself to smile. Anything to get out of telling her the truth.

"Mr and Mrs questions it is then. I want that prize."

And he did. A whole weekend at a top city hotel, meals included, just before Christmas? Very nice indeed. But more than that, he needed to distract her. Thankfully, for him, it worked. Perhaps, deep down, Lexie was also choosing to put his idiocy behind them.

Despite Callum's best intentions to lead her astray, Lexie stayed strong with her plan for them to keep clear heads, right up to the moment of the quiz itself, with her only allowing him to get them a bottle of wine as they were about to be called up onto the makeshift stage in the main conference suite of his company's office block.

"We mustn't look like we're trying too hard," she whispered as they made their way up and collected the paddles on which they would display their written answers, holding them up simultaneously.

In the end, it didn't look like they were trying at all.

First song you danced to together? *When you're looking like that*, by Westlife. Not romantic, but why would it be?

They'd been in the union nightclub with Callum's course-mates in the middle of their first term, enjoying a break in their studies with a big night out, and Callum had pulled her onto the dancefloor when he saw her eyes light up at the first few notes of her favourite song.

What was she wearing when you first met? Pyjamas. The less said about that, the better, given the circumstances of their recent encounter. The last thing Callum needed when he was trying to concentrate was to start picturing Lexie in her nightwear. Or his.

Where does he most want to travel to? Australia. But the truth is he won't, because he's scared of spiders.

What is her proudest moment? Winning a Young Environmentalist of the Year Award for an essay on recycling when she was still at primary school. She still kept the award on her desk at work.

If he could take only one thing to a desert island, what would it be? His mobile phone. They both knew Callum wouldn't last an hour without needing to check something.

Who is the better cook? Slight hesitation. Callum. Lexie was more adventurous, but in terms of technical skills, she wasn't a patch on Callum.

Again, and again, question after question, each one answered correctly. Callum looked about him as genuine couples who had been married, or at least together, as long as he'd known them fell foul of what he considered straightforward questions. Beside him, behind the podium, Lexie reached for his hand, giving his fingers a slight squeeze.

"We're so close," Callum muttered, picturing the luxury hotel suite, wondering what event he could celebrate with it. And who with.

"So everyone keeps telling us," she replied.

He realised Lexie had misunderstood him, but then, didn't she have a point? Didn't every-one? Mark's comment once again rushed into his mind, but he refused to be side-tracked now. Three more questions answered correctly, and if their opponents got even one wrong, the prize was his. Theirs. No, his; it was his party, after all, and his client they were there to impress.

Who is more obsessed with their phone? Callum. Too easy, given the response to the desert island question.

If she could meet one celebrity, dead or alive, who would it be? Sir David Attenborough. The fact that she'd be too nervous to say anything was beside the point.

The final question: Who is the better driver? A moment of panic. They had to get this one right, but what was the right answer? In the end, both opted for honesty. Both and neither; not a driving licence between us.

The silence from the audience told them the winner wasn't clear-cut.

"Well," the host was saying. "An interesting situation. Couple A have put different answers, whilst Couple B have the same, even though they haven't given a name. But, by the rules of the game, consistency is key, so on that basis, the winners are… Couple B!!"

"That's us!" Lexie squealed, turning to Callum and throwing her arms around his neck in joy. Without a moment's hesitation, he reached around her waist and spun her around, to the delight of the watching crowd. As he put her down, her face was bright with happiness, the look he loved so much on her.

"Where would I be without you?" he whispered into her ear, squeezing her tightly in gratitude.

It was only as they approached the host to claim their prize of the hotel voucher that it got awkward.

"How about a celebratory kiss for the cameras from our winning couple?" the host was asking, as Callum held the envelope aloft to the cheers of his own team of colleagues, watching on from the front of the audience.

The cries of agreement and encouragement from the crowd at large gave them no choice. Callum raised his eyebrows in question to Lexie, hoping that despite everything, for the sake of the crowd, she would agree. He needn't have worried; she was clearly still giddy from the win, and without hesitation, leaned in and brushed her lips against his.

It was over in a matter of heartbeats, but for that fleeting moment, all Callum could think about was the fact that it was the first time they had kissed where mistletoe hadn't been involved. Through hand-holding, plenty of dancing, even waking up in his bed, had there really never been a non-Christmas kiss? He pulled Lexie closer with his free arm, deepening their kiss, to louder cheers as she responded in kind, until she ended it, pulling away, although not so swiftly as to raise any doubts of their coupled-up status. Looking at her, he was certain the confusion he could see in her eyes was mirrored in his own.

As the crowd began to drift away, back to the bar, dancefloor or buffet, Callum and Lexie stayed almost motionless, still clinging to each other, on the stage. His heart was racing, and he was certain hers was too.

"Congratulations, Mr Fitzpatrick," she said, reaching up and kissing him on the nose.

"Congratulations to you too, Mrs Fitzpatrick," he replied, pleased she had made the first move.

"I think we've earned that wine," she said, gesturing to the almost untouched glasses, standing beside the still-half-full bottle on their podium. Pulling her arms away from him, she sauntered over to retrieve her own drink and the bottle, nodding to him to collect his own. "Come on. I suspect we're about to get torn to pieces by the ones who know the truth about us, so we might as well get it over with."

Callum collected his own glass and followed her back into the bar, his mind full of what had just happened.

SATURDAY 16TH NOVEMBER

Lexie

Staring into her wardrobe, Lexie felt uninspired for the first time in as long as she could remember. She was usually so good at this part of the 'going out' process, but tonight, nothing seemed to fit the bill. Possibly because she wasn't entirely sure exactly what the 'bill' was. True to his word, Mark had got in touch earlier in the week, asking her out, and in exactly five hours' time she would be meeting him at the Natural History Museum's ice-rink. There was a strange fluttering of nerves in her stomach that she hadn't experienced in a long time. Finally, the forecasted temperatures forced her to settle on sensible, and she pulled herself together. She could do this. Whatever 'this' was. Sensible jeans and layers. She may not be the worst ice-skater in the world, but she was nowhere near proficient, and if she was going to fall over, there was definitely the need for extra padding.

However hard she had tried, even once she knew she had a date ahead of her, for the past week Lexie's mind had been dominated by thoughts of Callum. They had caught up mid-week for a coffee after work, but conversation had been dominated by how well their win

43

had gone down in Callum's team, rather than anything about the event itself. She had kissed him! In front of everyone! Something had taken over her, and she hadn't even bothered pretending to fight it. Moreover, he had kissed her back. Just thinking about it was making her head spin, stirring up old feelings that hadn't troubled her for so long.

However hard it was, she had to force thoughts of Callum out of her mind for the night. After all, she had a date...

"So, you and I hold first and second place in the rankings of Cal's friends," said Mark, smiling across at her, as they moved slowly around the edge of the ice-rink. They were playing it safe, allowing the chatter to continue as they went.

"Yes, and you're solidly top of the league. I'm practically a late-comer, only meeting at eighteen, compared to, what, five for you?" Lexie's plan not to think of Callum was going well. Not.

Mark nodded. "He always says you rescued him, the night you first met?"

Lexie smiled and shook her head at the memory. "That old story. It was nothing. The second night of uni, there was a party in another hall of residence that everyone had gone out to, but I'd come back early to call my boyfriend, so was relatively sober compared to everyone else when they rolled in a few hours later. I was sitting up reading, and suddenly heard somebody slump against my bedroom door. As I opened it, Cal literally fell at my feet." She laughed as she pictured the moment when Callum had tumbled into her room. "He could barely stand, so I dragged him inside, leaned him up against my wardrobe, and forced him to drink what was left of the coffee I'd been drinking. He was in no fit state to be left alone, so once he'd managed to drink another coffee and a pint of water, I put him in my bed, and sat up until he came round in the morning."

"He wasn't in a good way when he left for uni." Mark squeezed her hand as they made their way around the end of the rink.

"No." Lexie knew all about Callum's state of mind back then. Newly-dumped, he had gone off the rails in spectacular fashion when suddenly free of the binds of living at home. That's how she had recognised him when he fell through her door; the previous evening she had seen him bouncing around the place, introducing himself to anyone he met, clearly trying to become the life-and-soul of this new party he had found himself at. The exact opposite to her approach, which had centred around calmly and quietly introducing herself to her new neighbours, and deciding to see where that would take her. She had accepted Callum's eager handshake, introduced herself, and watched him spin away again. On the Monday morning after the party, knowing there was nothing planned other than a tour of the campus, Lexie had let Callum sleep, and when he woke up, full of sheepish regret and profuse apologies, she had walked him back to his room and plied him with more coffee, and they had spent the whole day talking, sharing every aspect of their lives. From that day on, they had become inseparable.

"All these years of friendship, but you never dated? The one girl immune to the charms of Callum Fitzpatrick." Mark chuckled. "You must have some sort of super-power; I'll wager there are plenty of women who would buy it from you if you could bottle it."

Lexie suddenly found her feet to be of great interest and studied them intently. How was it that she was out with somebody who could easily be described as exactly her type, and all they were doing was talking about Callum? And at Mark's instigation too. The whole thing made no sense. She felt herself falling into the usual story as to why they weren't together, despite what the universe seemed to want for them. "When we met, I had a boyfriend, whilst Callum was freshly-single, and very keen to take advantage of that fact. Then, when I was single, he wasn't, beginning a constant back-and-forth that lasted for years. We were simply never in the right place, romantically, at the same time. So, yes, perhaps there was an element of attraction at the start, reciprocated even, but it wasn't right. We respected each other's boundaries. And then, one day, it just wasn't a factor anymore." Or at least not one they discussed any more, and one which hadn't troubled her for ages until the other evening. "But come on, we should not be talking about Callum; we should be enjoying this lovely evening."

That was when she made her mistake. The simple gesture to the surrounding rink was just enough to throw her off-balance, and her feet flew out from under her. In an instant, she felt a pair of arms wrap around her, steadying her before she could go crashing to the ground. Mark's arms. Strong, secure, safe. Too safe. What Lexie didn't feel, as Mark kept tight hold of her, guiding them both smoothly to the rail, making sure she had a solid grip before loosening his, was any sense of thrill. No rush of excitement as his hands moved gently from around her waist. No quickening of her pulse as their eyes met. No sparkle of emotion as she thanked him for having kept her upright.

"Are you all right?" Mark looked straight at Lexie whilst she gathered herself.

"Fine," she muttered, pulling her jumper back into shape. "Just fine. But perhaps this is a sign; time to head for somewhere with more stable ground?"

"Sounds good to me," Mark replied, grinning. "I know a cosy little place, just around the corner."

They strolled along in companionable silence, but Lexie's mind was buzzing. Glancing across at Mark, she could almost have laughed. After so long without even the hint of a date, she'd just been the sole focus of one of the cutest guys she'd met in years, and yet had felt... nothing.

As hard as she tried to force it from her mind, all she could think of was a comparison of Mark catching her as she slipped, and Callum's arms around her as they kissed up on the stage after their competition win. It was ridiculous.

"Here we are."

Mark's voice broke into her thoughts.

"My favourite bar in London. So far, at least – it's still early days. But it's the nicest so far."

He had good taste, Lexie thought, as she looked around Mark's choice. Despite the mid-November chill, the open-air terrace bar was indeed cosy, as he had promised, thanks to an impressive number of patio heaters, and she found them a quiet corner, surrounded by fleece blankets, as he went to get their drinks. When he returned, Lexie (determined to forget her moment of confusion earlier) focused hard on Mark, leaning in closer to hear him better as he told her more about his new advertising role, the job which had brought him back to the UK. He was charming, that was for sure, and had plenty of stories from his years abroad to keep her amused. Several drinks later, though, the chill in the air had turned decidedly frosty, and as Lexie returned from the toilets, she was dimly aware that it was time to head home.

"I think it's time we called it a night," she said to Mark, folding the fleeces into a tidy pile beside her on the bench. She looked across at him, as he nodded in agreement.

"Thank you for a lovely evening; it's been a pleasure getting to know you better," he replied, a smooth coolness in his voice as he stood to help Lexie on with her coat.

As she turned to say the same to him, Mark leaned in, kissing her gently on the lips. His actions did nothing to calm the turmoil in Lexie's mind, as she found herself responding, deepening their kiss, enjoying the sensation of feeling attractive, desirable, and the centre of Mark's world. The sensation didn't last long, doubt creeping into her mind even as she broke their kiss, and pulled away. But despite her misgivings, she found she couldn't quite let go of Mark's arms, and was pleased to find he felt the same way. "Would you like to come back to mine for a coffee?" she whispered, before she could change her mind.

He grinned back at her. "I think that would be an excellent idea."

Callum

It was a punishment, thought Callum, as he paced his living room once again, looking at the clock, and knowing it was only a matter of hours until Mark was going to be taking Lex out for a drink. She might have said she'd forgiven him for his stupidity in causing their argument and letting her down, but clearly she hadn't, and now, an evening out with his oldest friend had somehow been weaponised. Or at least, that was how Callum was seeing it. Lexie hadn't been on a date for ages, so why the sudden change of heart now? Add to that the fact that she had kissed him at the end of the quiz, yet despite her reassurances mid-week, she was clearly still seeking to punish him. Well, two could play at that game. He reached for his phone.

"And you genuinely didn't know you had been at school together?" Two hours later, Callum was forcing as much enthusiasm into his questions as he could, desperately trying to keep his focus on Amanda, the beautiful blonde whom he had picked, shamefully, based solely on the fact that she was the first girl in his Contacts list that he knew for sure was single, and most likely to accept his last-minute offer of a Saturday night out. Not his finest hour; even he knew that.

And however stunning Amanda was, however hard Callum tried, his mind kept wandering to Lexie and Mark. Were they having as hard a time as he was, trying to keep up conversations in which he had no interest whatsoever?

Somehow, it didn't seem likely. If he knew them both as well as he thought he did, their conversations would be flowing as easily as Callum expected the drinks to be doing as well, if they headed to the bar, as Mark had suggested they might, later in the evening. That thought in itself was driving him mad. Knowing how unfair he was being to Amanda, after one more drink, he did the appalling trick of faking an urgent phone call, made his excuses, and walked her to the nearest station before heading home alone. His reasons for being out with Amanda weren't remotely honourable, as Lexie's warning to remain a rogue, rather than tip into being a sod, rang loud and clear in his mind. Whatever his reputation, Callum Fitzpatrick was not a bad person, he just wavered from time to time when he encountered an attractive woman.

Unable to settle even once he got home, he poured himself one whisky, then another, and another, until he crashed out on the sofa.

The next morning, there wasn't the usual hint of a hangover in Callum's mind; there was a full-on sledge-hammer attack going on inside his head. It took him a whole ten minutes to work out where, exactly, he was, having fully expected to be waking up in the smart town-house he vaguely remembered Amanda sharing with a couple of friends. He mustn't have made it that far. Unless he had made the terrible error of inviting her back to his? A slow, careful search of his apartment showed that at least he hadn't made that mistake.

Sunday, then. A whole Sunday ahead of him. No plans, nothing to worry about; he could just curl up in a ball on his bed and feel sorry for himself. Or he could do what he usually did on a Sunday, and head to Lex's. If he was going to feel sorry for himself, he might as well be doing it with company. The image of sharing a strong coffee at Lex's breakfast table flitted into his mind. Yes. A quick – no, a slow – shower, and he'd head around. That would make everything better.

Almost as soon as he turned his key in the lock to Lexie's flat and entered, even in his fragile state, Callum could sense something was different. Wrong, even. There was nothing obvious, just an uncomfortable sensation as he made his way through the hall and into the living room, calling out as he did so.

"Morning, Lex? You up and about yet? I brought croissants." It had seemed the least he could do, as he'd strolled past their local bakery and been tempted in by the smell of fresh baking. Chocolate and hazelnut; her favourite combination. When no answer came, he headed to the kitchen, noting the sound of the shower running as he passed the closed door of the main bathroom. Odd for her to be using that one in the morning, rather than her own en-suite shower-room, but it was her house after all; she could use whichever of her bathrooms she liked. "I'll pop the kettle on," he called in the vague direction of the running water.

"Cal? What the... What are you doing here?"

Callum turned, to find Lexie standing in the door to the kitchen, the door to her bedroom wide open across the hallway. It took him longer than it should have done to notice she was still wearing her pyjamas, and that he could still hear movement in the bathroom. "I... I was hungover. I brought breakfast. Thought we could use your good coffee, pretend we're in Paris."

Her eyes widened as the bathroom door finally opened.

"I'll have to come and use your shower more often, Lex. It's far better than mi— Oh. Callum. Um. Hi."

It was all Callum could do not to drop the jar of coffee beans he had pulled out of the cupboard. "Mark. Um. Morning. Hi." He looked at Lexie, then back at Mark, his head suddenly spinning again, having recovered slightly on the walk between the two flats. Finally, he took in the dazed look on her face, her tousled hair, and the fact that she was still wearing the remnants of what must have been last night's make-up. He realised now what had been odd in the hall – a pair of men's shoes, and a man's jacket hanging up alongside the usual coats on the rail. How had he not noticed that? "I… Yes. I should go."

Without even stopping to say goodbye, Callum pushed past Lexie and Mark, rushed back through the hall, and out of the door, ignoring the lift for the speed of the stairs, as the hazy memories of the night before flooded back. Lexie had been out with Mark. That's why he had the hangover. He'd been trying to forget. Well, that had worked. Too well, as it happened.

Only when he was back in the safety of his own home did Callum dare stop his hurry. Heaven knows how many people he had barged into in his urgency to reach the flat, but as he leaned back against his closed front door, he closed his eyes and tried to think straight.

Lexie and Mark. The image of them together seemed to be burned into his eyes. He'd never felt this way when he'd known about her other dates. What had gone so wrong this time?

Maybe, troublingly, Mark had been right in his theory about Callum still being attracted to Lexie after all this time. Trust Callum to realise it at exactly the wrong moment.

SATURDAY 23RD NOVEMBER

Lexie

Five text messages. It wasn't often Lexie could remember the exact number of times she had been in touch with Callum over the course of a week, but this time she could. And they weren't even long messages. Three had been that very morning, to confirm whether he still want-ed her to go with him to his office party. As the same client was hosting them this year for Christmas and Bonfire Night, they had reached the mutual conclusion that it was probably for the best that they attend together, having won the Mr and Mrs competition just weeks earlier, but Lexie certainly wasn't looking forward to it, and she suspected Callum wasn't either.

Beth had joined her for a morning's shopping and lunch, and they were now sitting in Lexie's bedroom, enjoying a glass of wine, when Lexie finally managed to get Callum on the phone.

"So, long time no speak?" She tried to sound casual.

"Sorry Lex, I just... Well, you know. Are we all right?"

Lexie thought about it. Were they all right? It had been a shock when he walked into her flat the Sunday before. No, that wasn't right. Him walking into her flat on a

Sunday morning wasn't a shock at all. Him finding another man, and Mark of all people – that had been the shock. For him as much as it had been for her. The awkwardness after his departure had stretched out for a full hour, as Mark tried to make light of the situation, making coffee and dishing out the croissants, but in truth, part of her had wanted to rush around to Callum's and explain exactly how things had been. But of course, she hadn't. She had made it to his street, even to the door to his building, before her nerves had failed. What on earth had she been intending to say to him anyway? In the end, she had settled for all but avoiding him the rest of the week. Clearly, he had opted for the same.

"We're fine." Or they would be. She hoped. "Just tell me what the plan is for tonight. I mean, the invite you sent me said 'smart casual' – what are you going with?" She was once again rummaging in her main wardrobe, phone wedged between her ear and her shoulder.

"Ooh, a casually open-necked shirt, that navy suede jacket, and a tartan scarf." Beth threw herself back on Lexie's bed, where multiple pairs of trousers had been lined up for potential pairings.

"Shush." Lexie glared at Beth. "If he's wearing a scarf, the open shirt is pointless, and it's due to snow, so suede would be ruined. Cal? Talk to me." She listened as he rattled off his plans. "Right. Grey trousers, blue jacket, jumper, shirt. OK. I'll match you, it'll look good. Your dark purple jumper yeah?" Lexie pulled a patterned dark purple shirt out of the wardrobe, and held it up to Beth. "This? With matching jumper, navy jeans, brown boots? Hat and scarf for a splash of colour?"

Beth nodded, then stood up to start browsing Lexie's jewellery collection.

"I'll leave you to it then, Cal, and what, see you at the north gate at six?"

He mumbled his agreement, and she hung up the phone.

"So, Alexandra, what is it that you're not telling me? This one?" Beth held up a chunky silver necklace that would sit just inside the collar of Lexie's jumper and shirt. "And this?" The matching bracelet was also held aloft.

"Yes, that'll work. And I don't know what you mean." Despite having invited Beth around with the sole intention of sharing what had happened and seeking her advice, now that the opportunity was there, Lexie somehow couldn't face it. The fact that her friend was still infatuated with Callum didn't help.

"Please. It's been a week, and you've not mentioned either Mark, which is odd, or Callum, which is downright bizarre."

Lexie took a deep breath, and decided to get it over with. "Callum came round on Sunday morning. Mark was, sort of, still here."

"Still he— Oh, LEX! Yes!" Beth squealed, before reaching for her wine glass and shifting to sit crossed-legged on the bed, clearly ready for a dose of gossip.

"It's not what you think. Well, I suppose it is, but also not."

"You're talking in riddles, my friend, and not making sense. How did Callum handle it?"

Lexie relaxed for a moment; her friend had gone to straight what mattered to herself, and skipped over the potentially awkward truth of the matter. That it really wasn't what she thought, or what Callum had immediately assumed either. "He ran out of the door like we'd set fire to him. But he left the croissants behind as he fled, so at least we had breakfast."

"And you're still going out tonight? Won't that be a little, well, difficult, if you're seeing Mark? You are seeing Mark, right?" Beth was sitting up again, her head tilted to one side, like a quizzical cat.

"I'm sure we'll bump into each other now and then," said Lexie. It was true, at least; there was indeed every chance she'd be seeing Mark again. Just not in the context

Beth was imagining. "Look, anyway, that's the situation. Which means that although we're going out to his party tonight, Cal won't be joining me for our usual 'getting ready' pre-party, and why I needed a second opinion."

"Well, I think you'll look fabulous. Although I still think Callum should send us a nice snap of himself, once he's ready, just so we can make sure you're not clashing…"

Laughing, and grateful that Beth had broken the possible tension around the situation, Lexie grabbed the nearest cushion and threw it across the room at her.

At ten minutes to six, under a heavy grey sky that was threatening at best snow, and at worst a storm, Lexie approached the north gate to the park, her stomach in knots. This was ridiculous. She had known Callum long enough by now, surely? It had been a shock, yes, for both of them, she was sure, but there was no point now in dwelling on the events of the previous week. And tonight wasn't the moment to tell him what had actually happened between her and Mark. Or rather, what hadn't. Tonight, they had to put on a good show to his employers and clients, and continue to be the prize-winning couple of a few weeks before. They could do this. She could do this.

Callum was waiting dutifully at the entrance, looking as handsome as always, just as Beth had anticipated. He certainly did scrub up well, even in smart-casual. He'd done particularly well this evening, Lexie noticed, and for a moment, her confident self-talk faltered. Could she do this?

He turned and grinned at her, running a hand through his hair. "You're here."

"As promised. And look, I do think we should talk about last weekend."

"No, we shouldn't. I should never have come over. I knew full well where you were, who you were with, and what might have happened, I don't know what came over me. Let's just pretend it never happened, and have a good evening?"

It wasn't a good idea, but it was Saturday night, it was cold, and the warmth of a heated marquee was far more appealing to Lexie than standing outside potentially starting another argument. She put her arm through the crook of his elbow and let him guide her towards the party, pleased to at least have made that first physical contact with him. She hadn't realised how much she'd missed him.

"Is there anything I need to know this evening?" she asked, as they drew closer to the venue.

Callum shook his head. "Same client as Bonfire Night, and the usual crew from work. Nothing to worry about. And it isn't even a formal party, hence we're here, rather than the usual hotel ballroom." Pausing, he reached for her hand. "This isn't a 'Mr and Mrs Fitzpatrick' event, all right? I was hoping this could be a 'making things right between us' event, where I could ply you with good food and drink, and we have a good time. How does that sound?"

Lexie nodded. "That sounds like just what we need."

In the end, Callum was only half-right, and the party was exactly as Lexie had known it would be all along: Callum's colleagues (or at least the ones who knew very well that they weren't an item) joking about their success at the Mr and Mrs competition, and those who didn't know they were just friends commenting on what a perfect pair they were. Lexie bit her tongue, knowing how important it was for him that these people were impressed. And she could do 'impressive' just as well as Callum could when she needed him. Her journalist's brain was wired to remember critical things like names of spouses and children, where peoples' favourite holiday destinations were, or even which restaurant they had mentioned intending to try, the last time they had met. The two of them really were unstoppable when they put their minds to it.

Tonight, Callum finally introduced Lexie to the new project manager he'd been talking about for months. Davie. Husband to Sarah, father to twins, a boy and a girl, just about to turn two. Lexie had done her homework, as she shook hands with Davie and Sarah, chatting merrily away about local schools, and the importance of reading bedtime stories to little ones as they grew up.

Callum

Lexie was in her element, thought Callum, as he returned to their table with a tray of drinks. All he had to do was get through the evening without making a fool of himself, and per-haps, just perhaps, they could put his idiocy of the previous weekends well behind them. It was troubling, though; this was the second time in as many months he had done something stupid and almost jeopardising their friendship. He had to be more careful. Even a week of not speaking to Lex had shown itself to be torture; if they ever fell out for real, he wasn't sure how he'd cope. Suddenly he realised what he'd admitted, if only to himself. The shock almost caused him to drop the tray, if Davie hadn't stood to help distribute the drinks at that exact moment.

"Honestly, Callum, I don't know why we don't see more of Lexie. We should definitely all get together for dinner one evening.".

"That would be lovely," agreed Lexie, accepting her glass of wine with a smile. "Callum and I went to The Citizen for my birthday last month, and it was just perfect."

"The Citizen?" Sarah looked across at Davie, her eyes wide. "Well, that has to be on our agenda, that's for sure. The four of us? It would be fabulous. Always good to have an excuse to get the glad-rags on, hire a babysitter, and treat ourselves."

"And you deserve it. Callum's told me how hard Davie

works, and it can't be easy keeping on top of everything like you do." Lexie looked up at Callum. "Let's get a date in the diary, once the Christmas madness dies down?"

Callum nodded, a broad smile on his face. There was always a tinge of regret when these things were organised, that he was, essentially, lying to people, and hoping that none of his colleagues would let the truth slip. It was even worse, this time, knowing that Lexie was certainly dating somebody else. Wasn't she? He needed to know. Deep down, he didn't want to know, but he had to find out the truth. "I agree, completely, but for the moment, do you mind if I borrow you?"

A flicker of doubt flashed across Lexie's face, but she rose, said goodbye to Davie and Sarah, and followed him to a quiet corner, glass in hand. "What's up?"

"Are you and Mark dating?"

She blinked at him. "What? I thought we were pretending last week hadn't happened?"

Callum ran his free hand across his face. "I can't. Or at least, I can't until I know if I'm actually out this evening with another man's girlfriend. My oldest friend's girlfriend at that. It doesn't feel right."

"You aren't."

"So, you and he…"

"Are just friends. We had a pleasant evening, and that's all there is to it. But don't worry, there's no bad feeling, no bitterness, and we won't be at each other's throats if we're ever in the same place again. Quite the opposite; I think we'll become the best of friends."

Callum stared at her. "Better than us?"

"Well, you introduced us, you're just going to have to take that risk, aren't you?" She smiled at him, reaching up to stroke his cheek. "Seriously, Cal, have some gumption. You are my best friend, you always will be. As I hope I'll be yours; after all, who else would put up with you?"

It was enough to break the tension that had been present between them all evening, despite their best pretence to the contrary. Ignoring the awkwardness of them both still carrying their drinks, Callum pulled Lexie towards him into a one-armed hug, holding her as closely as he could, given the circumstances.

"Come on, we have a party to wow with our wonderful display of coupled-up bliss." She wriggled out of his grip, put both of their drinks on a nearby table, and took his hand in hers, before gesturing towards the dancefloor. "Shall we?"

Callum let himself be led, his head suddenly far lighter than the two small glasses of wine would have caused. Lexie and Mark weren't an item. The news filled him with an odd mix of glee and horror. Dancing in front of his colleagues, he realised the pair of them looked more natural in each other's company than half of the actual couples that surrounded them. Could it really be that easy? Maybe tonight, he should attempt to find out.

Two small glasses of wine hadn't made him drunk, but another shared bottle's worth later, and neither Callum nor Lexie could claim full sobriety. Neither did either of them care, as the spirit in the marquee had somehow both lifted and calmed, everyone now having let their guard down and relaxed, once a few of the more senior managers had made their excuses and departed. Lexie leaned into him as they retreated to one of the cosier sofa areas, collapsing together in a fit of giggles.

"Do you want to head home?" he asked, gently raising her chin so he could look her in the eye, see as well as hear her reply over the buzz of the room. She was giddy, as he was, but certainly not drunk. Still more than capable of deciding if she had had enough of keeping up the 'entertaining and devoted girlfriend' act for the night. She smiled at him, and nodded. It was only as he went to stand up, he realised her arm had found its way around his waist, holding him in place. "Lexie?"

"I don't know how good an idea this is, Cal, but,

well..." Then she kissed him.

Lexie

Lexie didn't remember waiting for their taxi, or arguing about whether to go to her flat or Callum's. She forgot about how she'd fumbled in her bag, her keys suddenly having vanished somewhere into an inner pocket or lining. She didn't remember Callum laughingly reaching for his own set to her building, and them both desperately trying to be quiet as the exact same thing happened at her own flat's front door. Those things didn't come back until the next morning. They didn't matter at the time.

What mattered as they stood in the gently-falling snow was the taste of Callum's kiss, the mix of red wine and dark chocolate. In the taxi, the heat of his body against hers as their kisses deepened, despite the obvious tutting from their driver, was seared into her memory. When her keys disappeared, she remembered the reassuring squeeze of Callum's hand, telling her it would be all right, that he would fix her problems.

Lexie remembered tumbling onto her bed, still strewn with clothes from her decision-making earlier that day. She could never forget the rush as they tugged at each other's clothing, removing everything as quickly as possible, not even bothering to clear a space. She could recall perfectly every moment, until they eventually fell asleep, entangled in each other's arms. And she would never forget waking up in Callum's arms the next morning.

Or at least, she woke up expecting to be in Callum's arms the next morning. Instead, she found the other side of the bed, and the rest of her flat, empty.

SATURDAY 30TH NOVEMBER

Callum

"You slept with Lexie?!"

Callum bowed his head, grateful the bar was practically empty. The incredulity in Mark's voice was deafening. "We didn't mean to. It was after the party. We'd had a few." It sounded terrible, even after a week, to say it out loud.

"And?"

"And what?"

Mark paused to take a swig of his beer. "Well, you've clearly told me for a reason, which means you want me to ask questions. So – 'And?' is my question. And… how was it? And… will you be doing it again?"

Both very good, and very valid questions, Callum had to admit. Questions he had been asking himself for the past week, highly aware of the irony that the one person he wanted to discuss it all with was the very person he couldn't talk to this time.

"OK. One, I didn't ask how it was for you, so you're not allowed to ask how it was for me. Don't you think it's already weird enough what's happened the last two weekends? Two, I have no bloody idea."

"Do you want to do it again?"

Another good question. If Callum answered truthfully, then it would give away his answer to Mark's first query. There was no other way. "Yes. But I don't want to be the one to say it." Because saying something could risk losing the great thing that he and Lexie had had all these years. Was anything worth that? Even something with the potential to be wonderful?

"Coward."

"Yup. Can we talk about football for a bit now?"

"No, this is too important. I wasn't going to say anything, but as technically you brought it up, and not me, there's something you need to know about the Sunday you walked in on me and Lexie."

Callum held his hands up. "Please, mate, no. It's weird enough that you're the only person I can talk to about this; I don't want to start thinking about you two as well. Even if what had happened between us hadn't happened, she's still my best friend, and I do not want to hear about her sex life. Especially not when it involves my other best friend."

"We didn't sleep together."

"What?"

It was Mark's turn to gaze into his pint. "Well, we slept together, but we didn't sleep together. A hell of a lot of snogging, God, it was great, like being a teen again, but by the time we got into her bedroom, we were both shattered, having second thoughts, I think, and just, crashed out in her room. We slept together. Literally. For half the night anyway; I woke up around four and headed into the spare room. And then you showed up with breakfast. Which was great. Embarrassing, massively awkward, but great."

Callum stared at his friend. "She didn't say." She hadn't. Not one word. Lexie had let him go a whole fortnight thinking she had slept with Mark. She'd slept with Callum himself, whilst letting him think she had slept with Mark. What the hell did that mean? Lexie had never seemed the sort to play games. Things may have been awkward, but they had been in touch, and spent the entire evening at Callum's Christmas party acting relatively normal, giving Lexie plenty of chances to say something. "Does she, oh hell, does she remember that nothing happened? She doesn't think you had some crazy night together?"

"Oh no, she remembers. She apologised."

"Apologised?"

"Didn't want me thinking her either a slapper or a tease. One, for taking me home, two, for nothing happening. I assured her I thought she was neither. I had a cracking night. Although clearly, not as good as yours."

There was no response to that. But Callum knew he had to confess the rest.

"Trouble is, though, I wasn't there in the morning. There was no luxurious breakfast for us."

"What? What did you do?"

"I panicked. I bolted."

Without another word, Mark shook his head, downed his pint, and left Callum sitting alone, contemplating the stupidity of his actions. Again.

Lexie

"You slept with Callum?!"

Lexie could see the excitement shining in Beth's eyes, but couldn't tell if it was at the prospect of Callum and her finally being a 'thing', as Beth had implied she wanted to see for years, or at the prospect of juicy gossip about Cal's reputation and prowess. She wasn't sure which would be easier to deal with.

"How was it? And how have you not mentioned this all week at work? This is your biggest personal news in years, and you've said nothing?"

Lexie stared at the wine glass in front of her, wondering whether sharing the news with Beth had been the smartest plan. But then, who else was she going to talk to about this? The obvious usual option wasn't available this time.

"Well? I'm waiting. Now, come on, you know we all fancy Callum, and Tams has remained annoyingly tight-lipped about her couple of months with him. Oh no!" Beth's eyes widened. "Is he absolutely terrible? Sexy to look at, but then nothing to write home about?"

"No! He's… He's… He's good."

"Only good?"

"All right. He's very good. And that was with alcohol involved." There was no point lying now. Callum was indeed as good as all the girls had imagined him being.

"Bet he'd be excellent sober then. So why, exactly, aren't you out with him tonight, and getting the chance to find out?"

Lexie didn't know. Well, one reason was that she hadn't heard anything from Cal since Sunday morning. Another, equally valid, reason was that she hadn't made any attempt to contact him in the meantime either. The friendship they had shared all this time was special, however silly that might have sounded to anyone else, and the last thing she wanted to do was throw it all away by engaging Callum in a conversation it was clear neither of them wanted to have. It just needed time. Then it would be all be fine. Or at least that's what she kept telling herself.

"I don't even know what I'd say to him," she admitted to Beth, suddenly finding the label on the wine bottle utterly fascinating.

"How about '*Hi, are you free tonight?*' as a starter-for-ten?"

Lexie shook her head. "It's not that simple. I mean, we've been friends forever; we were both angry and confused leading up to last Saturday. It was just a stupid mistake, I'm sure."

"I know you. And I know Callum. If this had been a stupid mistake, then you'd be out with him right now, and then we'd all be making daft jokes about what happened. One of us would probably buy you a joke wedding certificate for Christmas as a laugh. But no, you're skulking in the Hart with me, and," she reached for the bottle, "destroying the label of this poor bottle of wine. At least tell me what happened the next morning."

"Nothing. He'd gone when I woke up."

When Beth didn't reply, Lexie looked up, unsurprised to see the look of horror on her friend's face. It was the same look she'd seen in her own mirror the previous weekend when she realised Callum had vanished without a trace. "I think that tells you everything you need to know, don't you? But, it's for the best."

"Explain how you've come to that ridiculous conclusion?"

"Beth, I've just turned thirty. I love my job, I have a great little flat in a lovely area, and I have wonderful friends. I'm settled in so many aspects of my life, it's time I thought about settling down romantically too. I've been thinking it for a while." Lexie wouldn't admit that sometimes, just sometimes, it was Callum's face she saw when she imagined her future happiness. "If last weekend proved anything, it's that Callum Fitzpatrick is not going to be part of that. Otherwise, why would he have run away? If it was meant to be, he would have at least stayed for breakfast so we could have put things straight." She had hoped saying it out loud would convince her of that fact, and help soothe the pain that had settled in her heart for the last week.

"You could always go back to Mark."

Lexie laughed. "Yes, well, there's something you need to know about that night as well…" It was time to come clean on that topic too. By the time she had finished telling the sorry tale of her Sunday morning drama with the two best friends, Beth was visibly torn between hysterics, fury and sympathy, her face a picture of pure confusion.

"You've managed to get yourself stuck in a love triangle without even trying, my friend, and a particularly complex one at that. I am going to get us another bottle, and when I get back, it's up to you whether you want to dissect it further, or switch topics." Beth leaned forward to gently kiss Lexie on the top of her head. "It will all be all right, I promise."

Lexie wished she had the same confidence.

SATURDAY 7TH DECEMBER

Callum

Callum had nearly called Lexie at least six times a day, stopping himself just as he was about to hit Dial. Mark was right; he truly was a coward. Eventually, he did hit *Dial*. But it wasn't Lexie's number he selected.

Beth answered almost immediately. "Callum? Are you after Lexie?"

"Hello? What? No. No, I, um, wondered if you fancied a drink tonight? Maybe a bite to eat?" He half-hated himself for asking, but as he was holding his phone, it had seemed such a good idea. A test, almost. She was so similar to Lexie, as Mark had been so keen to point out, that he needed to find out, one way or the other, exactly why he had been avoiding the situation for so long. He could almost hear Beth at the other end of the line, thinking his question through.

"A date? Tonight?" She sounded cynical. He didn't blame her.

"Yes, why not?"

Beth paused. For a moment, Callum considered laughing it all off, claiming it was nothing but a joke, then she continued. "All right. Where and when?"

"White Hart? Eight? Nothing major, just a couple of casual drinks and dinner." Already he had lowered what he had been aiming for. In the space of less than a minute, his offer seemed to have reduced from a full-on date to just a casual night out. At this rate, the whole thing would be completely cancelled in another minute. Perhaps that would be for the best.

Another pause from Beth. Callum started wondering if she was even on her own; what if Lexie was standing right next to her, hearing everything? Finally, she spoke.

"I can do eight at the Hart, sure. I'll see you in there – best get us a table booked, mind. I'll leave that to you."

It was a challenge, he suspected. He could easily call her back in an hour, claim there hadn't been any availability at the Hart, and used the excuse to cry off altogether. It was strange, Callum thought, the number of possible ways-out he was already planning into everything, or that Beth was leaving open to him. He knew she liked him, and had done for years, so why would she be hesitant now? Lexie. It had to be Lexie. Had Lexie confessed all of what had happened after the party? If so, then who knew what was going through Beth's mind? Certainly nothing good about him; that much could be guaranteed.

"I'll let you know when I've got it booked, and see you this evening," he found himself replying.

"I'll look forward to it," Beth assured him.

Callum wasn't sure he would.

Lexie

As hard as she tried, Lexie couldn't remember a time when she and Callum had gone this long without seeing each other, unless one of them had been physically out of the country. A whole fortnight. And likely longer, given there hadn't even been a call or text since 'that night'.

When her phone beeped to let her know she had a message, she was ashamed at how quickly she reached for it, and that she felt a wave of disappointment that it was Beth, not Callum, who was getting in touch.

Beth: *Are you free to talk? x*

She replied: *Of course, what's up?*

She barely had time to close the message app before the phone rang.

"Beth, is everything all right?"

"Callum's asked me out tonight. I've said yes." Her friend's words came out in a rush, as though she was saying them quickly, before she could change her mind.

"He's… what? I mean, OK, that's, that's fine." Lexie was painfully aware of how high-pitched her voice had become on the last word. She coughed and cleared her throat to try and get back to her normal tone.

"Really? It's really fine?"

No, Lexie thought, it wasn't fine, and she wanted to scream that down the phone at her friend, and then tear around to Callum's flat to find out what the hell he was playing at, and why he wasn't asking her out, after what had happened. But she couldn't do that, could she? Not when she was just as guilty of not asking anyone out. This was the 21st century; she no longer needed to wait for Callum to do the asking. If this was his decision, it was his decision, however much she might hate it. "Look, Beth, I know I told you what happened, but if Cal's asking you out on a date, then it's very clear that in his eyes, we're just friends." With focus, her voice sounded just about normal. "That's the way it is, and that's that. If anything, it helps prove the point that he isn't the man I'm supposed to be with." The tone might be normal, but as she said the final few words, Lexie could hear her voice starting to crack, as tears threatened to flow.

"You're not going to fight for this?"

Was she going to fight for it? Was there anything to fight for, if Callum was already asking one of her best friends out for a date? Maybe it was some kind of sign; that they were so far into the 'friend zone' that even having slept together wasn't going to change anything. She cleared her throat again. "No, I'm not going to fight for it, because there's apparently nothing to fight for. I hope you have a lovely evening, truly I do. But, maybe, don't feel the need to tell me about it immediately afterwards, all right?" She hoped Beth would blame the sound of her voice on nothing but a crackling connection.

"I'll tell you everything that happens, all right?"

"No, Beth, please; I really don't need to hear that. It's bad enough hearing about half the dates he goes on with strangers, but hearing about one of my closest friends? That's pushing things too far." Even as she said it, she felt the sadness hit her like a physical pain. If she had thought the previous week was opening a door to something, she was clearly wrong. This week, that door was being firmly closed, bolted, and a chair jammed up against it for good measure.

As she hung up, after Beth's assurances that there'd be no gossip, Lexie sank into her sofa, suddenly unsure how on earth she was going to distract herself on what had managed to become potentially the most stressful evening of her life. How could she and Callum have ruined things so spectacularly, just as it could have gone so perfectly?

Callum

Feeling proud of himself for not crying off at the last minute, Callum walked into the main bar of the White Hart, and almost had to catch his breath. As he approached the table he always reserved when meeting Lexie, it took him a moment to realise it was indeed Beth, and not Lexie, sitting in her friend's usual spot. Purple shirt, black jeans, silver jewellery: Beth was the spitting image of Lexie from the night of 'the incident,' as he was now referring to it. Even her hair was styled the same as Lexie had been wearing it the night of the Christmas party, tied up into a high ponytail, held in place with a glittery black scrunchie. Looking more closely, of course there were subtle differences: the shirt was plain, not patterned, and the jewellery was delicate, rather than the chunky styles Lexie always preferred, but there wasn't a chance this was a coincidence. Beth had been at Lexie's when she was getting ready for their night out the previous weekend, so of course she knew what outfit had been chosen.

"Beth, you look lovely, as always; that colour looks great on you." There, that should do it, thought Callum, as he greeted her with a kiss on each cheek. Should be enough of a hint to let her know he was onto her. And if it was a pure coincidence, then so be it. She did look lovely, after all. It was just a shame he was picturing somebody else in her place.

"Well, you did say 'casual', and I've not worn this shirt for ages. Can't imagine what made me think of it this evening, but there you go." A sly smile around the corners of her mouth, which didn't quite reach her eyes, told Callum that he was right; there was definitely game-play of some sort involved here. "Have you seen Lexie this week?" she asked as she settled back into her seat.

The sudden mention of Lexie wasn't what Callum was expecting. Having the woman in front of him looking so much like her didn't help the jolt of pain which rushed through him. "No, haven't seen her since we… since we went to my Christmas party. Why do you ask?"

"Just, she hasn't mentioned catching up with you for the last couple of weeks now; I wondered if anything was wrong?" Beth's face was a picture of innocence.

"Not that I know of. It's been a busy couple of weeks; we just haven't had time to see each other. I'm sure things will be back to normal after Christmas. So, drinks? What do you fancy?" He really hoped the Beth he knew would spark into life soon, make a flirtatious joke he could bat back a sharp response to, break the ice, move on. He might not fancy Beth, but he truly did like her as a person, and under normal circumstances, would happily have enjoyed a couple of drinks out with her.

"Martini. Surprise me."

"Right. Do you want to order some food at the same time?" He wasn't going to back down from this, whatever Beth was up to. He had promised her food and drink; she was going to get food and drink.

"Start with a starter? Always a good option. Fish goujons for me, if you please."

Lexie's usual, Callum noted, as he nodded and headed to the bar, his head spinning. When he glanced back, he saw Beth had instantly pulled out her phone. Texting Lexie? He didn't what to think what would be in the messages, if that was the case. Clearly, Beth was making her point by reminding him of Lexie. Callum would have to fight fire with fire, and be his most charming, to prove the tactic wasn't working. He didn't want to think about how ridiculous the whole scheme sounded: neither of them wanting to be there, but both determined to demonstrate how keen they were. How far, exactly, was he willing to go, to prove his point? And what exactly what the point he was aiming to prove?

He placed the Espresso Martini down in front of Beth, hoping she would notice the subtle hint of him having bought her coffee, implying it would be a long evening, and took a sip of his Long Island iced tea. Not his favourite, but a longer drink, again, to prove the point. If she was game-playing, then so would he. "So, are you all set for the big Christmas party next weekend? A sexy little outfit already planned, if I know you?" A gentle bit of flirting wouldn't hurt, to kick the evening off and see which way she jumped.

Beth took a sip of her Martini, and smiled approvingly before answering. "Naturally. Tams and I hit Regent Street last weekend. Lex cried off; not sure why. Maybe she already has something in her wardrobe she can give a second chance to, and doesn't need something new at all."

Was Callum imagining things, or did she narrow her

eyes at the mention of second chances? Just how much did Beth know? When he didn't respond, she continued.

"Either way, I can assure you, whatever she's wearing, all three of us will be looking suitably stunning. Perhaps you'll get the chance to find out, if you're lucky?"

"You don't have a date lined up yet?" He wasn't taking the bait of her implied assumption that he'd be turning up with Lexie as usual.

"I thought perhaps I'd see how this evening went. What do you think?" Beth paused as she stirred her cocktail, her eyes not leaving Callum's.

What Callum initially thought, to his shame, was that perhaps going to the party as Beth's date would give him the best chance of making sure Lexie had to see him. Caught off-guard, she might even speak to him. But no, that was too underhand, surely? Although, not as underhand as going out with her best friend the weekend before what was usually one of their biggest nights of the year. Callum's moral compass had clearly been derailed somewhere along the line, these last two months. "That seems a very sensible plan," he replied. "But anyway, enough about next weekend, let's focus on the present. How has work been?"

The subtle shake of Beth's head suggested annoyance at his change of topic, but suddenly, all Callum wanted to do was get the hell out of the Hart, and back to the sanctuary of his own flat. Whether Beth was playing a game for Lexie's benefit, or here of her own accord, he certainly wasn't intending anything romantic to happen with her. It would feel too wrong. Beth was a friend, that was all, whereas Lexie was a friend and so much more. Why else would he hurry to hers whenever he got the chance, in or out of a relationship?

As the moment of realisation struck, it drained the life out of Callum. He only wanted to be with Lexie, this evening, any evening, every evening. Suddenly he didn't have the energy to even have a friendly chat with poor

Beth.

Somehow, he managed to drag a conversation out of them both throughout their starters, but all Callum could think about was how he could politely but quickly get away.

"So, any interesting stories being covered at work? Any exciting developments in fashion?" He sounded false, and he knew it.

Beth played with the stem of her glass, as though debating how to answer. "We're doing an interesting series on relationships at the moment," she eventually replied. "The intricacies of friendships which look like they're turning into something more, even if the two parties involved always seem unable to see it for themselves."

Callum almost choked on his drink. "Right." What else could he say? He had to assume she was talking about him and Lexie, but what if he was wrong, and Beth was trying to hint about their own status? "Are you working on that one then?"

"A relationship, or the series?"

"Either?"

"The series, yes. A relationship, who knows how these things can suddenly develop?"

Callum knew. What he didn't know was how to continue the conversation. What on earth had happened to Callum Fitzpatrick, smooth-talker extraordinaire? He had known Beth for years, flirted harmlessly with her for most of that time, and never stumbled. Tonight, he was a wreck. Lexie. It was all Lexie's fault. "There's got to be the worry about ruining the friendship, hasn't there? Not wanting to lose the good thing you've already got? Is it worth the risk for a couple of nights of passion, if you end up without the thing you value so highly?" His words came out in a rush.

"What if it ends up being so much more than a couple of nights of passion, though? You have to take the chance, surely?"

Callum couldn't answer this time.

Evidently sensing his reluctance to continue the conversation, Beth swirled her glass, contemplating the final remnants of her cocktail.

"Did you want another?" he found himself asking, to break the silence, but hoping that she wouldn't.

"You know, I'm actually not in the mood for dinner," she said, looking up at him through her thick eyelashes. "I wondered if you fancied a night-cap, back at mine? I happen to have a very nice single malt I'm sure you'd appreciate far more than I would."

"Actually, I, um, I should have said at the start, I got an urgent call from work just before I left the flat. Turns out I need to work tomorrow. Early start, bit of a breakfast meeting, it turns out."

"Well, if that's the case, my place is nearer your office than your own, isn't it? Nice and convenient, you might say…" Her voice trailed away as her eyes stayed locked into his, leaving nothing to chance in Callum's mind.

It was definitely a test now, he thought. This wasn't the Beth he knew, but he knew why this version was here. This was a ridiculous challenge, a fight neither of them wanted to win, but one where neither of them could admit defeat. "No," he said, "I'd better not; I never can say no to a single malt, and it's a very important meeting, which I really don't want to mess up, if you know what I mean. I'll walk you to the Tube though?"

"I don't think so, Callum," she said, a glint in her eye. "You'll walk me to the taxi rank, wait with me until I get in a cab, and then pay for my fare home, like the gentleman I know you are, somewhere deep inside."

She'd won her battle fair and square, thought Callum, as he nodded and smiled, before standing to help her into her coat, but he was starting to see he could win the war if he got his act together. But he had to act soon. A plan started to form in his mind; he just hoped he could pull it off.

Lexie

Lexie woke up to her phone beeping on her bedside table: *He bolted after one Martini and the mini fish fingers. Just so you know. See, I waited a whole 10hrs before telling you* □ *B x*

Callum had bolted? Being half-asleep didn't help, but all Lexie could feel was an even greater sense of confusion.

SATURDAY 14TH DECEMBER

Lexie

Not even playing the cheesiest Christmas songs available at full blast all day could lift Lexie's mood, as she tried to convince herself to enjoy getting ready for her office Christmas Party. She knew she shouldn't be thinking about Callum, but whatever she did, there he was, popping up in the back of her mind.

This was officially a record now for lack of contact, and it was driving her mad. Thank goodness she had been busy at work, or there was a risk her days would have been spent staring out of the window, wondering just how exactly they had ended up in this mess.

Callum and Lexie. Lex and Cal. Their names had tripped off everyone's tongues for so long, a natural pairing when any event was being organised, easily partnered if formal dinners were being arranged, always relied on to bring the other if an extra body was needed for a particular activity or occasion. But just when had they slipped from being the closest of friends to becoming practically co-dependent? Three weeks since they last saw each other, last heard from each other, and Lexie for one was feeling like a part of her was missing. So many times, when she had been out and about, even scrolling through the news at work, something had caught her eye, made her laugh, or reminded her of Callum, and she'd pulled out her phone to call or text him, only to pause as her finger hovered over his name. Was he doing the same? She hated the fact that she was wondering. Even the simple act of not ringing him had played a cruel trick on her. For so long, he was at the top of her 'Just Messaged' or 'Just Called' phone history, and yet, after three weeks of nothing, he had slipped down the list, even out of the top ten for her call list. It was like their friendship was fading away, like the darkest point of a time-travel film, as photographs and memories begin to disappear.

This was ridiculous, she thought, finally pulling herself together, and knowing there was no point delaying things any further. In a flurry of determined activity, Lexie reached into the wardrobe and pulled out the dress she intended to wear. The same one she had been wearing the night he had surprised her with dinner for her birthday: black with long lace sleeves, just the job for a winter's night out. Her birthday. It had been the perfect evening. Easy. Straightforward. Comfortable. Was that a place to start a relationship from, comfortable? A sudden laugh escaped her at the thought of a relationship of any sort with Callum. The notorious ladies' man, a different girl practically every month – could he be boyfriend material even if he wanted to be? Was she patient enough to find out? As she had said to Beth, it was time for her to be serious about things, to be considering settling down. Callum Fitzpatrick was not the settling-down sort. Where would she even begin with changing that? And if she did change him, would he still be the Callum she adored?

But now, seeing the dress lying on her bed, she couldn't help imagining how it could be the evening of his Christmas party, in an alternative universe – one where either they had never slept together in the first place, or they had fallen happily into a relationship the very next

78

day. Croissants and coffee either way, but in the latter scenario, rather than lounging on her sofa, they could be snuggled up in bed, reading the Sunday papers to each other, enjoying their little in-jokes, not a care in the world. Whichever way it had gone, he would have been arriving at her door later this evening, looking suitably Bond-esque in his tux, ready to make her the envy of all the girls when they walked into the party arm-in-arm. Or was Cal, even now, staring at his planned outfit, just as Lexie was staring at hers? Was he still intending to turn up, as they had planned months ago in the middle of the summer, when the date of her Christmas party had first been announced, and she'd told him he would be needed, tux and all?

She knew she needed to know, one way or the other. But one thing she still wasn't ready for was to hear his voice, just in case hers gave way whilst replying, if she didn't get the answer she was hoping for. Lexie reached for her phone, holding her nerve steady this time, ignored the message history that had gone before, weeks ago now, and tapped out a message: *So, work party for me to-night... Do you have any plans?*

Hardly committal, and certainly not desperate; if he said he was busy, she could easily claim she was simply asking about his plans. As a friend. Nothing more.

Ten minutes later, the beep of a reply: *Out tonight myself. Somebody special.*

Before she had even finished reading, another messaged came through: *Enjoy the party.*

And another: *x*

'Somebody special.' Well, that told her everything she needed to know, didn't it? Still, she had to reply, had to appear fine with everything. Perhaps this was their first step back towards friendship. She hit reply: *Hope you have a good evening; at least the tux was ready... x*

So that was that. Switching the Christmas tunes for some nineties nostalgia and turning up the volume even further, Lexie pulled together her makeup for the evening, then headed for the shower.

Three hours and one taxi ride later, Lexie arrived at MacAndrews London, the location for this year's Christmas party. Only one block away from the office, it was their usual haunt at Christmas, booking out the entire ballroom, and a couple of adjacent rooms for food, or enjoying a quieter moment. She tried to ignore the fact that it was also the very hotel she had helped Callum win a two-night stay at, the very next weekend. In less than seven days' time, he would be walking through the very doors she was about to step through, no doubt with some lucky lady by his side. It should have been her. It so nearly could have been her.

Unsure what to do for a moment, Lexie hovered amongst the crowd on the street below the entrance, watching as a couple of colleagues from another floor appeared, giggling amongst themselves, gave her a quick wave and headed past her into the building, where one of the receptionists was waiting to direct them to the cloakroom. Everyone was in their finest, and clearly looking forward to having a good time. Was it really her first Christmas party since moving to London without Callum by her side? Was that tragic, or actually a good thing for her? It wasn't as though she would be entirely alone any-way. Beth and Tams would be there – she knew that much from their conversation during the week – and both were looking forward to a good evening out. It would all be fine. Of course it would. She had her girls.

Slowly, still not sure she wanted to go through with it, she climbed the stairs, holding back to allow a couple of others to head up quickly and into the lobby. She was being silly now. Knowing she couldn't stand on the steps any longer, Lexie straightened her shoulders and turned to push the door open.

"Lex."

Callum. Her hand froze on the handle. *Somebody special,*

his text had said. Could he possibly have meant her after all? Or had he been stood up again, and a random party with Lexie and her colleagues was better than a night in on his own, after he'd gone to the effort of going out? Frustratingly, Lexie found herself not caring. She had wanted him to be there, and there he was. Suddenly, another alternative struck her: was he here for Beth? Had their date the weekend before gone better than Beth claimed? Perhaps Beth had only been trying to spare her feelings – or worse, claim all was well before turning up with Callum tonight? Would Beth truly be that cruel, after all their years of friendship? Would Callum? She realised she had paused in silence for too long.

"Lex, please?"

"What do you want, Cal?" She turned to look at him properly, not exactly sure what she was expecting, but certainly not what she saw. He must have read the surprise on her face as she took in what he was wearing.

"You said it was black tie; I thought I'd come prepared, depending on how the next part went," he said, gesturing at his attire, and giving her a slow twirl.

Indeed he had. She'd seen him in black tie before – of course she had, at countless parties over the years – but now, on the street below her, there was something different about him. Her objective opinion, that he was 'handsome, but just as a friend', certainly couldn't stand any longer. His eyes seemed to burn into her soul in a way she'd never experienced before. She could see why Beth was constantly ogling him, that was for sure. Why almost every woman she knew was constantly asking after his relationship status. This way trouble lay, and she knew it. So why did the flicker in her heart suddenly increase at the thought of what he might be talking about?

"What next part?"

"Do you trust me?"

"Always, tragically." She always would.

Callum held out his hand, and smiled. That smile. Lexie

had always known it could be dangerous, but had somehow hoped she would remain immune, whatever the circumstances. It appeared she was wrong. With a swift longing glance indoors, where she could see glasses of champagne being handed out to new arrivals, Lexie shook her head, pulled her coat more tightly around her, and headed down the steps to where he was waiting. The jolt as their fingers entwined surprised her. Theirs had always been a tactile friendship, so why would holding his hand make a difference now?

Without a word, he grinned and started walking along the pavement, pulling her along behind him.

"Where are we going? Cal, I have a party to go to," Lexie protested, but didn't pull away from him.

He didn't reply; he just kept walking, giving her no choice but to follow.

They stopped at the end of the alley leading down the side of the hotel. With a squeeze of her fingers, Callum dragged her between overflowing bins, stopping underneath the flickering green light of a dingy fire escape.

"Would you say this was a romantic spot?" he asked, finally turning to face her properly.

Lexie couldn't help laughing. "What? No. No, of course it isn't."

"Good."

Holding both her hands in his now, she could see a nervousness in his eyes that hadn't been there before. He kept glancing towards the end of the alley.

"Cal, what is it? What's going on?"

He shook his head. "This was meant to be the easy bit, and now I feel like I'm having to build up courage. Should it be like that? Shouldn't it be easy? All natural, flowing, like it is in the films? I suppose they have people writing this for them. I've only got me. And you know me. That's the problem I suppose. I know you know me."

He was rambling now, and Lexie's heart began to race. This was it, then. One way or another, their future was going to be decided based on whatever happened in the next few moments. The trouble was, she still wasn't sure herself which way she wanted it to go.

And then it happened.

"Screw it. Here we go."

Before she had chance to remonstrate with him for his poor choice of words, Callum took a deep breath, pulled her closed, and kissed her.

And the world went on hold.

Callum

As she pulled away from him, breaking their kiss, Callum desperately searched Lexie's eyes for her answer to the question he had been too afraid to ask out loud. For a moment, neither spoke; neither even seemed to breathe. Suddenly a blast of music from a passing car distracted them both for a heartbeat, breaking the spell.

Lexie laughed, and buried her head in Callum's chest, her whole body shaking. Unsure exactly what his next move should be, he gave in to instinct, and wrapped his arms around her, holding her tight.

"What is it?" he asked, when the shaking didn't stop, and he was unable to tell if she was still laughing, or if tears had now taken over.

"Oh, Cal. Our first proper kiss is in a back-alley, and our song now appears to be *Cheeky Christmas*. Things really can only get better from here, can't they?"

Callum felt himself relax, slightly, although he didn't let go of her. He couldn't. "It's a 'yes' then, to us?" He needed to hear her say it. He realised he would never tire of hearing her say it.

Lexie stepped back, out of his arms, but took his hand in hers. "It's a 'yes'. But I think I would like it to be a 'yes' inside now, please, with champagne. And heating. And better music. And no bins."

"That sounds a fair deal to me." He must have looked

like a fool, knowing he was now grinning ear-to-ear, but he no longer cared. She had said 'yes'; that was all that mattered now.

"And one other thing."

He tensed. Was it all still a ruse?

"Our next kiss needs to be somewhere a lot more impressive."

Callum laughed and let himself be led back towards the main doors.

He knew he was being pathetic, but for the rest of the night Callum stayed as close to Lexie's side as she would let him. Drinks were refreshed, plates kept topped up with ridiculously small snacks, and colleagues charmed. He knew where his strengths lay, after all, and making sure Lexie came out on top in every conversation, no matter who with, was an easy win for somebody like him, used to crossing swords, verbally, with some of the best in the business. But despite it technically being no different from how he had behaved at so many of Lexie's work events, something was different tonight. For the first time, there was no pretence. And it felt wonderful.

It had been a calculated risk telling Lexie he was seeing 'somebody special' that evening. If he had arrived and found her arm-in-arm with somebody else, he wasn't sure how he would have coped. He couldn't have blamed her, after all. Mark would have been her obvious choice, and when the two of them had met up mid-week to watch the football, Callum had had to stop himself asking Mark if Lexie had been in touch. Lexie and Mark may not have slept together, but there was clearly a connection there, as friends even if nothing more, and Callum knew Lexie didn't always enjoy going to her parties alone. Worse, he had imagined finding Lexie with Beth, the latter drip-ping poison (or lies) into Lexie's ears about their so-called 'date' the previous weekend. Beth could have absolutely destroyed him in Lexie's eyes if she'd wanted to, but in all honesty, he knew Beth wasn't the type to be so malicious. Perhaps Beth and Mark should have a formal introduction after the Christmas socialising circuit was over, Callum found himself pondering, as he looked about for Lexie on his return to the main room after checking that the second part of his plotting was going to plan.

Lexie was nowhere in sight, but he headed to where he could see Beth and Tams chatting at the bar whilst waiting to be served.

"Ladies, have you ordered yet? Please, let me have the honour?" If he brazened it out, he might just be all right.

"Oh, smooth as ever I see, Fitzpatrick." Tams turned to him. "Yes, you can buy us drinks, a bottle of champagne I think would be only right, each if we're being honest, given the amount of angst you've caused both of us these last few weeks. She's been a mess. You must know that, even if she wouldn't tell you."

"Angst? I've been the epitome of charm, as always, I assure you." He tried in vain to catch the bartender's attention.

"Too much charm," chimed in Beth, a wicked smile on her face, and a mischievous glint in her eye. "She knows, you know, that you asked me out, then cut-and-ran after two drinks and the starter. And after I'd put *so much effort* into my choice of outfit."

So Beth had definitely been playing him, then. Callum was almost relieved. "I thought you looked particularly enchanting that evening; there was definitely something about you," he replied, keen to let her know that he had been onto her from the start.

"Bad form, Callum, bad form." Tams shook her head. "Trying for three out of three, were you? Shocking."

"So, are you here this evening as Lexie's boyfriend, or merely Lexie's friend-that's-a-boy? Believe me, there is a right answer." Beth was standing with her arms crossed now, looking as menacing as she could whilst also wearing a bright pink cocktail dress and a tinsel-draped tiara.

"Well, I know which I'm trying to work towards, I can say that much; in terms of which I'm actually here as, that's up to Lex, not me." He may have had her declaration in the alleyway, but things could change; he wasn't going to take anything for granted, not this time. Seeing the lady in question weaving her way through the crowd to their group at the bar, Callum felt himself tense. He was more than aware of his reputation, but being around three women he had either been involved with, or almost been involved with, and who he knew were the closest of friends, sharing everything, did not fill him with joy.

"Oh, Cal, the look on your face, it's a picture of pure panic." Despite her words, Lexie's eyes were dancing, a bright smile lighting up her face as she slid her arm around his waist, her eyes dancing as he responded by pulling her in even closer. "Are you two ladies being my defenders, ensuring his intentions are correct?"

Beth looked Callum up and down again. "I don't think this boy has had a correct intention in his life."

"Maybe not, but I swear I have one now, or at least, I'm doing my best to develop one." He reached for Lexie's free hand, and raised it to his lips. "I was going to buy these two a bottle of fizz – did you want a drink, or a dance?"

"A dance. We can have a drink any time we like, from now on."

"From now on. Yes, I like the sound of that." He bought the champagne for Beth and Tams, then joined Lexie on the dancefloor. Joined his girlfriend on the dancefloor, he corrected himself. Yes, he could get used to this.

As the night drew to a close, Callum put the next part of his plan into action. Waiting until Lexie returned from the cloakroom with her coat, and finished saying goodbye to the girls, he blocked her path when she headed to the doors, one hand behind his back. "I may have forgotten to book us a taxi home."

She blinked at him. "But you weren't meant to be here; I've got my own booked."

"Consider it cancelled."

"Callum…"

"You did say our next kiss had to be somewhere more impressive." Taking her hand, he pressed the object he had been concealing into her palm.

"What? 'Duchess Suite'? Cal, what have you done? I don't have any other clothes."

Ten minutes later, despite the cold, their next kiss certainly was significantly better than their last, standing on the balcony, a bottle of champagne awaiting them on the table and Lexie's overnight bag from Callum's in the bedroom, with some of the best views over the London skyline.

SATURDAY 21ST DECEMBER

Callum

"Screw it. Here we go."

Callum did his best to glare at Lexie, but it was a challenge when he knew he was grinning like a fool. "You're going to use that whenever you open, start or otherwise 'do' anything from now on, aren't you?"

She grinned back at him, and threw open the door to their hotel suite. The Royal Suite. Their prize from the Mr and Mrs competition, this was even more luxurious than their Duchess Suite the previous weekend. Little had either of them imagined they would be legitimately using their winnings as an actual couple.

"I am indeed. Until you give me something better to talk or think about."

Callum could think of plenty of ways to distract her, not least the particularly stunning piece of jewellery that had drawn his attention as he walked home from work two nights ago. It had taken him all of half an hour from seeing it in the window, to placing the order; as much a surprise to himself as to the sales assistant, who had been delighted at such a decent sale so close to closing time.

He would definitely make a better job of getting that

moment right in their relationship. Callum Fitzpatrick, despite claiming to anyone who would listen that he was a contented bachelor, a ladies' man through-and-through, with no intention at all of ever settling down, had found his mind drifting for the last couple of days. It was all so clear – the setting, the mood, the question. Hopefully, he could imagine her answer too, because he had even been able to picture their Big Day. In a way, it was a good thing the ring would take a few weeks to arrive, although he didn't intend to wait another decade. One week into their burgeoning relationship was certainly pushing it.

For now, he took her hand and pulled her towards the bed.

The End.

OCELOT PRESS

Independent authors publishing together.

Thank you for reading this Ocelot Press book. If you enjoyed it, we'd greatly appreciate it if you could take a moment to write a short review on the website where you bought the book, and/or Goodreads, or recommend it to a friend. Sharing your thoughts helps other readers to choose good books, and authors to keep writing.

You might also like to try books by other Ocelot Press authors. We cover a range of genres, with a focus on historical fiction (including historical mystery and paranormal), romance and fantasy.

To find out more, please don't hesitate to connect with us on:

Website: https://ocelot-press.com

Email: ocelotpress@gmail.com

Twitter: https://twitter.com/OcelotPress

Facebook: https://www.facebook.com/OcelotPress

ALSO BY JENNIFER C. WILSON

The Kindred Spirits series (Darkstroke):
Kindred Spirits: Tower of London
Kindred Spirits: Royal Mile
Kindred Spirits: Westminster Abbey
Kindred Spirits: York
Kindred Spirits: Ephemera

Through Ocelot Press
The Raided Heart
The Last Plantagenet?
A Novel Approach

Printed in Great Britain
by Amazon